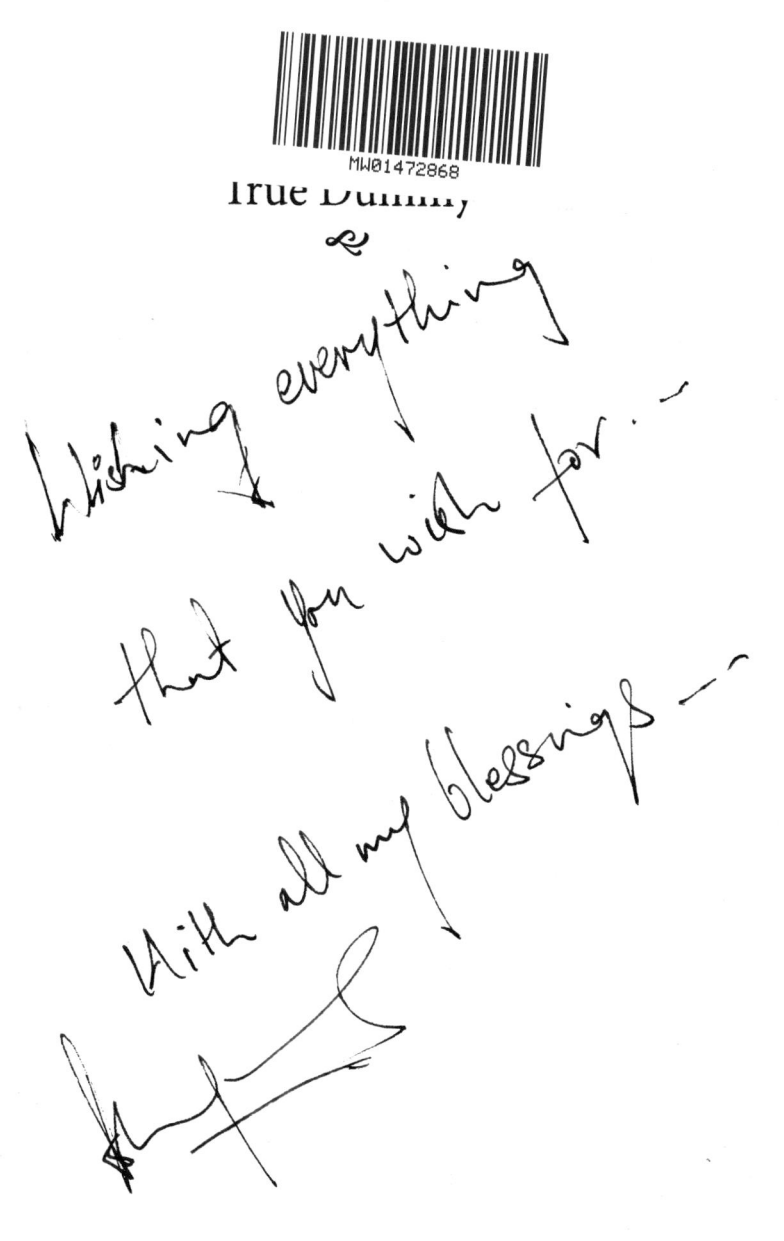

True Dummy,

Wishing everything
that you wish for...

With all my blessings —

True Dummy
A fable of existence

Ashish Jaiswal

Rupa・Co

Copyright © Ashish Jaiswal 2009

Published 2009 by
Rupa . Co
7/16, Ansari Road, Daryaganj,
New Delhi 110 002

Sales Centres:

Allahabad Bangalooru Chandigarh Chennai
Hyderabad Jaipur Kathmandu
Kolkata Mumbai

All rights reserved.
No part of this publication may be reproduced, stored in a retrieval system, or transmitted, in any form or by any means, electronic, mechanical, photocopying, recording or otherwise, without the prior permission of the publishers.

The author asserts the moral right to be identified as the author of this work.

Typeset in
Mindways Design
1410 Chiranjiv Tower
43 Nehru Place
New Delhi 110 019

Printed in India by
Nutech Photolithographers
B-240, Okhla Industrial Area, Phase-I,
New Delhi 110 020, India

Acknowledgements

~

For, whose name is written on every fragment of mine – Pooja, my wife.

Because of who, I am – My parents, to them.

Smearing the soil of my country India on my forehead, I begin.

PART 1

PART I

One

'Be warned!' out came the untethered tongue of the old wanderess of the mela, throwing her caustic voice onto my back; her long nails pressing hard on my reluctant young shoulder. 'One step further in the future and you lose on life forever!'

My raised foot jammed, hearing what followed; my eyes froze on the crimson horizon, on the returning birds flying in the foreground of the dying sun.

What was she saying?

The most important break of my life, one which I was considering the best stroke of fortune, the base on which I had erected the castle of the future, according to her was nothing but one of the several wicked curses that destiny lays on a blind ant?

Yes, a blind ant. That is what I was, according to the rules of the mela; the one who got deceived by his unfaithful destiny.

It was not only I who was stunned by her verdict. Geoga, my childhood friend, too, remained seated on the dusty grounds with his eyes wide open as the old woman went on to reveal what the future had in store for me.

The sky was getting darker. The mela had started to fold up. If it were any other day, Geoga and I would have retreated to our village long back, fearing for our lives – the mystical wanderers of the mela were too fearsome for young village boys like us.

But not today.

Today, the old woman's revelation had defeated all the reasons for us to return to our changing village.

My head turned towards the far-standing hazy mountains, as my mind went back in time to the day my veiled destiny came knocking at my door.

~

'Mother, when will we see it?' I asked with subtle impatience, trying to keep my sleepiness at bay.

The cow was about to give birth and I could not wait to cuddle the newborn.

She just smiled peeping through the temporary curtain drawn in front of the stable. Afraid that I might accidentally look into the agonising eyes of the delivering cow, I quickly, though reluctantly, withdrew from the window.

Although always happy with the new arrivals, I could never understand why all of them had to be born at night and why did it have to be so painful for the poor cow?

I was scared of the dark.

How strange it was that everything that appeared saintly in the daylight turned into a demon-like creature as soon as night fell upon it – the mountain, the jungle, the trail behind... even Saviour sometimes? I wondered why Saviour wanted to carry on its course even during such fearful nights. Why could it not go into hiding like all of us?

The forceful wind of the night was compelling the only tree near my hut to screech. I slid further under my quilt and closed my eyes. After all, it was the perfect formula to scare the demons away.

My small village was hidden amidst huge mountains, which remained covered in dense clouds. Although majestic, the misty mountains isolated my village from the outer world making it difficult to reach it. Hence, centuries ago during the invasion, my village, like many others of the region, turned into a Christian refuge. Mother used to say, 'God feels safe in the mountains.' But I think, it must have been difficult for him to notice us from those mighty heights through that foggy drape, and why not? My village barely existed in that vast valley of yellow flowers.

The mighty mountains were hard to ascend; only the curious sheep went there. Like other children, I could at best climb the rolling hills that surrounded the valley. But even from the lesser hills the sight of my village was spellbinding – hundreds of tiny red-roofed huts separated by narrow white trails on one side of the Saviour and the stony ruins and patches of the mysterious jungle on the other; the old church was the only remaining structure on that side.

Saviour, the stream, truly divided the valley into two halves.

It could get tricky in our mountains, as digging the earth for water is impossible and people have to rely on the never-drying streams. Mother once said, as we all sometimes do, to focus on our thoughts and draw random lines on paper, God drew these streams on the stones when he was creating the earth. Saviour is what God sketched on our valley. Villagers relied on it and worshipped it for nurturing life and maybe, hence named it Saviour.

The aged church stood among the stony ruins, at the farthest end of the valley, mysteriously hiding the source of Saviour.

It is said that centuries ago our land faced a fearsome invasion. Nobody knew where these invaders came from, some said they were from the west, while others opined that they came from the desert. In spite of stiff opposition, these invaders kept marching ahead, burning houses, killing people.

Our valley, because of the mighty mountains, remained safe for a considerable period of time. But one day, in spite of the imposing heights, some invaders successfully crossed the peaks and landed in our peaceful valley. Frightened by the invasion, the villagers took refuge inside the church, while the invaders captured their houses, which, in those times, like the church, were built of stone.

Many days passed with the villagers locked inside the church without food and water, their death almost certain, when one day, suddenly, an earthquake struck the valley and destroyed all the houses including those of the invaders. Surprisingly, the church, although damaged a little, was saved along with the villagers. This stopped any further threat of invasion. Not only that, in the years to come, the church almost became a pilgrimage for Christian refugees.

As the stony ruins were difficult to remove, the villagers thought that it was wise to rebuild the village on the other side of Saviour.

The church remained as it was; where it was, now... slightly distant from the villagers.

Whenever I sat on the hills and looked towards the church, one thing that my young mind could never answer was, whether the church came first or Saviour, for, to me they both appeared to have existed since eternity. I had seen them both, together, right from the time I had opened my eyes in this valley, in the small red-roofed hut of my parents.

'Moo' announced the happy arrival of the calf but I had already slipped into the strong arms of dreams which almost always carried me away to the misty mountains.

※

To me, Saviour was a friend, the closest one. Near the church I even had my favourite rock, on which I would sit for hours talking to it. I used to study in a large red-roofed shed close to my hut. Thanks to my mother, who worked as a cleaner at the church, my schooling was free of charge at this missionary school.

When I was young, every morning my mother would dress me, comb my hair and drop me off at school on her way to work. But my mind always wandered during the classes and longed for her presence. I could never wait for school to get over so that I could run to the church to meet her.

Unlike many other children who sang in the village choir and who practised daily inside the church, I loved to spend my time near Saviour.

I was not meant to belong inside the church. My voice was not melodious enough. I remember my mother trying very hard so that I could learn to sing, but I was just not good enough. Besides, I never understood what the master meant when he always glared and interrupted my rehearsals asking me to sing 'from your stomach and not from your unholy mouth!'

I tried and tried, as my mother watched from the corner of her eye while cleaning the windows, but it was all in vain. The master always ended up in frustration, throwing his arms up in the air and shouting at my mother, 'Take this block of wood away, his voice can never reach God!' And my poor mother, scared of losing her job, used to rush down the stairs to take me away from his furious eyes. With her work still unfinished, she had no option but to ask me to stay beside Saviour until she was done.

I was more than happy to be with Saviour. I knew my mother liked it when I studied. And hence, to please her, I always pretended to read my schoolbooks when I was there. In order that she could hear, I read them aloud whenever she came out to check on me.

Never knew when my pretence turned into habit, when my hours beside Saviour grew longer and how, unknowingly, I went on to pass my examinations every year.

※

The mooing of the hungry calf woke me up earlier than usual. I rubbed my eyes and jumped out of bed to rush towards the stable. My father, as usual, sat at the door cleaning his paintbrushes. My village was too small to provide regular work for my father who was a roof painter. Although the times had changed, I still had memories of childhood when I accompanied him to his work carrying his paint tins and brushes and then rushing towards the hills to watch him paint the red roofs.

I loved the fact that most of the roofs in the village were painted by him. I used to proudly point out the newly painted roofs to my friends who in turn used to applaud me, as if I owned the houses beneath.

My father was a good painter but the roofs were few, soon, there came days when he was without work. Initially he went quiet but, as time passed, he became temperamental; even when he had nothing to do, he would wake up early and end up cleaning his brushes over and over again. It was often on the milk produce of the two cows in the stable and my mother's regular income that our family survived.

I halted, unsure of my father's temper. Surprisingly, he smiled and made way for me. The arrival of the calf had brought happy times – the cow was ready to give milk. I rushed towards the snow-white calf that ran in circles like a blind mouse, maybe hunger had made it go mad. Unable to chase it, I gave up and hurried out of the house to break the good news to Saviour.

Lost in my thoughts, I did not realise that I had reached the church. I was proud of the fact that I could walk on the white trails blindfolded; the village was imprinted in my mind. I crossed the wooden bridge and entered the broken gates. The church was silent as usual – its rusted bell that had fallen down was lying as it was in its yard. I walked towards Saviour, casually staring at the old structure – its long walls and the sloping roof were now totally covered with ominous wild creepers. It appeared as though the thick grove was not pleased with the only remaining man-made structure in its territory and looked desperate to engulf it. *The Church or Saviour?* The question hovered again in my mind.

I told Saviour about the newborn while removing the weeds that had grown along its banks. My rock was situated just where Saviour turned along the church and disappeared beneath the mountains. With all those thorny bushes and dark trees, it was the densest end of the valley... as if Saviour did not want anyone to come any closer and discover its origin.

To me, the wilderness was a hindrance; a blot. I kept thinking of ways to beautify the surroundings. Initially I thought of painting all the bushes red, I even tried it but it was too much of an effort. Then one day I got the idea of sowing flowers near the banks. I spent the next few days clearing the area around my rock and then sowing it with hundreds of flowers, which I had been plucking from the valley and preserving in the bushes. I kept dreaming the entire night about how those flowers would turn into fully blossomed plants the very next day!

I came home crying when my experiment failed. I still remember how, while I sat weeping near the stable, my father, who loved gardening, eagerly explained to me the process of creating plants from plants. I jumped with joy, as it was the way to fulfil my dream. After that, growing flowers and battling with the weeds along the banks of Saviour became my favourite activity.

Tired due to the effort, I sat on my rock. Saviour was quiet. Its serene water gently caressed my hands. I knew it was happy – it was always happy in my happiness.

*

A few days went by. The everlasting hunger of the calf had started worrying me. That night, I quietly watched my father and mother arguing – the cow was not giving milk and it did not seem as if it would. This was a big turn in the scheme of things. I stared towards the stable. Suddenly the calf started appearing unwanted; its arrival a curse.

Little did I know back then, that it was much more than that, it was the bearer, one that would change the course of my destiny forever. After all, if it were not for the calf deprived of milk, I would not have sat in my uncle's shop, would have never met the old woman from the mela, would have never played the game of pearls and maybe, would have never known ... why I needed to exist on this earth.

For a long time, father had wanted me to work for his brother, a well-to-do man who owned a rice shop at the prestigious Market Corner; mother was reluctant, as she feared it would disturb my studies.

I think the cow's failure had tilted the argument in my father's favour, the night ended with my mother finally agreeing but not before managing to convince him that the work should in no way disturb my studies.

Two

The Market Corner, catering to several surrounding villages, was set up as a detached area outside the valley, almost at its mouth. It was perhaps a wise economic decision to have it there rather than inside the valley, as lorries carrying goods could freely come and go. Moreover, I feel machines do not derive pleasure on the unexpected pebbly trenches as the live ones do.

I never saw vehicles moving inside my valley; at best, there were cart-horses and pushcarts, which would ferry goods into the village. However, there were signs of a wide road running from the Market Corner deep into the valley along the rolling hills straight to the old church. But now only an unpaved jagged path remained, covered with bushes for half of its length. I slept with excitement.

I liked the Market Corner, a bustling place, a place where everyone appeared clever – vendors as they knew exactly what price to sell at, and customers, at what to buy.

I loved sleeping till late but that day I was up early, even before my father. I got dressed up and sat at the door waiting for him, to make sure that he did not forget. I still remember how I kept walking ahead of him on that jagged path, eager to reach the Market Corner first, forgetting in my exhilaration that I was walking away from Saviour – little did I realise, back then, that I would end up this far away.

My small eyes rolled with excitement, admiring each and every piece of the Market Corner at length.

The wide circular space surrounded by shops of all types was bursting with life. Hawkers were sitting on the ground with old goods; farmers were standing with their pushcarts of vegetables and their goats. Sitting or standing, they were all luring buyers with their loud shouts.

An old, life-size, bronze statue stood right at the centre of the circular space encircled by constantly moving buses and lorries. Several small groups of people scattered all over the remaining open space were engaged in agitated discussions. I knew they were discussing important matters; after all it was not any ordinary crossing of the white trails but *the* Market Corner!

Unlike the noisy streets, the shops were calm. Shopkeepers, whether they were selling silk, rice or any other item, were sitting peacefully behind the decorative showcases and were looking out with relaxed eyes, as if not worried about their businesses. Perhaps the temporary footing of the street hawkers and poor farmers were no competition to their permanent shops.

And, in one such shop, sat my uncle. I was proud of the fact that his rice shop was one of the biggest in the Corner. Listening to my father's request, my uncle mocked; although being the younger one, my uncle always ridiculed my father for his lack of entrepreneurial skills. In the past, he himself had suggested to my father to bring me to him but my father always avoided it reluctantly as my mother would not let me go and now my uncle had a point to prove.

Least bothered with his scathing remarks, I kept glancing into the bakery next door – the smell of fresh cakes was too tempting. My father ultimately managed to convince my uncle.

He had to get convinced; after all he was a good businessman. In me he was getting a 'man from the house' – one who could be paid less yet could be trusted more.

୰

My first encounter with Geoga happened at the Market Corner itself. It was an intriguing sight – a burly man severely beating up a boy my age and a woman trying to intervene without much success.

Geoga's family had recently moved to our village. His father used to work as a travelling salesman, hence, often spent many months away from Geoga and his mother. Perhaps this was the reason why Geoga was often absent from school, something his father never liked.

My mother, who rarely came to the Market Corner, saved Geoga from his father and introduced me to him. From that day Geoga and I became friends. His father, who was always looking for reasons to beat up Geoga, spared him whenever he saw us together. Geoga's mother loved him a lot and to save him from his father's anger, often lied to him about Geoga's whereabouts. I tried hard to encourage Geoga to study but failed most of the time.

Geoga was like a wild bull – sticks or words, nothing could bring him under the yoke. His father eventually gave up on his dream of seeing his son become an educated man. He then tried to force Geoga to assist him in his job but, as if Geoga was completely oblivious to his family's poverty-ridden destiny, he simply refused.

Geoga always had expensive interests and big dreams, and yes, a mother to support, something that never allowed his father to relax.

It did not occur to me often, but sometimes I did compare my circumstances with those of Geoga's and wondered what relationship sincerity shared with destiny – was it because of my hard work that my father was out of a job or was it Geoga's playfulness that kept his father toiling?

※

It is said in our mountains that our destiny is a lazy creature, which hates to move. Whether it lives in a rich man's house or a poor man's hut, it matters least to it. I think both my uncle's and my father's destinies were lazy – my father's destiny was happy living in his poor house whereas my uncle's destiny was comfortable in his shop, which did brisk business.

Initially, I did not understand why customers who would quibble endlessly with street hawkers walk straight to our shop and happily buy goods at exorbitant prices. Later, I could attribute it only to my uncle's smart business skills and maybe to his *lazy* destiny.

I did not know that the day I set my foot in the Market Corner, my destiny decided to change its house but as it is a lazy creature, it took a few years before it really did that.

I liked sitting in my uncle's shop, I was impressed by his confidence, his control over life. Nothing unpredictable ever awaited him. He was so natural when it came to earning money that I sometimes could not help but compare him with my struggling father.

It was hard to believe that they were born to the same mother.

Soon, I learned how to look busy to the wandering customers, how to swiftly lure them into buying. I knew shouting and pleading like street hawkers was useless. In fact, it was the opposite. I realised people were more willing to buy when we convinced them that our business was not at all dependent on them and that it was entirely their need to buy from us. I also realised that people liked buying from shops that did well. They would happily queue up in a busy shop but would never go to a shopkeeper waiting to serve; maybe these customers were scared that seeing them alone, the poverty-ridden destiny of the idle seller might open its eyes and start to follow.

A few years went by.

My life kept revolving around my village and the Market Corner and I grew into a sixteen-year-old boy. Despite spending considerable time in the shop, my closeness to Saviour and my mother's persistence had helped me sail through my school life. I still remember the day when mother came running to the shop with the news of my admission to St. Gonava. Situated in the nearby town called Akora, St. Gonava was one of the best colleges in the area. It was a place where the sons and daughters of wealthy people studied.

Mother knew that studying at such a college was impossible for her son and the fact that a generous scholarship was covering the expensive tuition fee made her the happiest. My uncle, who was somewhat irritated with the news, underplayed his anxiety, as he would do with his reluctant customers.

My mother left quickly. She did not want to aggravate my uncle. She knew that fickle family circumstances still required me to work in his thriving rice shop.

I walked back home, slightly bemused. How awkward people like me are with good news! Our limited rehearsals fail us completely in situations where we have to respond, especially when it is something big.

I saw my father at the door with his brushes. 'You have made us proud,' he said, 'It is a blessing to have a steady source of income. You know, life in this village with its usual uncertainties is otherwise painful.' Although illiterate, my father knew that friendship with the rich students of St. Gonava was a surety to a decent livelihood. I smiled, I knew my village was limited in terms of opportunities and my years at the Market Corner had taught me that only the people who sold through permanent shops prospered.

I went inside the house and saw mother preparing supper. Seeing the thrilled expressions on her face, I realised that the cooking would take longer than usual. I found it a good opportunity to run to Saviour and break the big news to him.

∽

Geoga came to know about my selection a few days later. Now he often went missing from the valley, returning only when his father was not around. Nobody knew where he spent his time and with what kind of people. I too never asked. This is how our relationship was.

He gave a hollow smile.

Although nobody could have guessed looking at his presentable attire, I knew he was having a tough time. His debts were mounting and had started narrowing his dreams. I thought of suggesting to him that he should join his father but refrained.

Our friendship was strong but not strong enough to let me step in his father's shoes.

~

Soon the day arrived. Akora being one and a half hours away from our village, I had to wake up early to catch the first morning bus.

'You look like a prince in this!' mother said, kissing my forehead. She had knitted a new woollen jacket for me.

I was pleased for my mother, often surprised by her confidence in me – her insistence with the choirmaster, her faith in my studies, her belief that I would be admitted to St. Gonava.

While staring at her, I remembered those two lines that were engraved on the damaged porch of the old church:

Fortunate are those who are trusted more by others than by themselves; blessed are those who trust others more than they trust themselves.

I felt fortunate. I smiled, as I took her blessings and left for my new journey.

'Like you, I too have never been out of our village!' I shouted joyfully to Saviour while leaning from the wooden bridge. Saviour was quiet. He looked like a sweet child with folded arms and swollen cheeks, pretending to be angry. 'Do not be impatient!' I teased Saviour, 'When I will come in the evening you can see Akora through my eyes!' I laughed and shouted while tossing a flower towards him.

'Goodbye, Saviour!'

The restful stream waved towards its banks.

I ran on the jagged path to reach the Market Corner, which was waking up for the day. The shops were yet to open but the hawkers and farmers had already arrived and were busy stocking and decorating what would be their 'temporary holds' till the evening. My classes were held on alternate days but I was, in a way, happy to be away from the Corner even if it was only thrice a week.

I grew anxious, as my bus swirled past the statue-rotary to move out of the valley. Like an ant, it moved slowly amidst those grey mountains, progressing carefully on the narrow tracks. Soon the mountains were replaced by rocky beds, rocky beds by green pastures, and green pastures by dwellings.

I was so mesmerised looking out of the window that I did not see that my destiny had already sneaked off and disembarked near the deserted rocky beds. Perhaps it knew that in the next few hours somebody would turn up exactly there to welcome it.

Three

~

My grandmother who died when I was young used to say that towns have a magical power to steal people's past and capture it inside a mirror. Once people enter and settle in towns, they can only run towards the future. Exasperated, at times they stop and look behind, their heart wanting to return, only to find that their parents, their childhood friends, their village are now all inside a mirror that they can only look into but can never enter.

Akora was not very big yet it was magical.

My bus moved through the paved roads, garlanded roundabouts and wide bridges but my eyes did not; they just stared out of the window at those fascinating buildings, colourful vehicles and groups of attractive young people – all of them laughing, all so confident.

St. Gonava was grander than anything I had ever seen, I had ever imagined – the big arches, the imposing towers, the adorned cupolas! I entered its embellished gates admiring those hundreds of impressive men and women all engrossed but all too engaged to welcome me. Then I remembered my father's advice to make friends with my rich classmates, and one look at them convinced me that they would definitely become the links to my secure future.

Walking through the broad corridors of St. Gonava and comparing it to the narrow trails of my village, I reached my new classroom where everyone was keenly occupied in introducing themselves.

I paused for a while, slightly hesitant, and then slowly became a part of them. Standing at the rear, I peered through their shoulders, as they introduced themselves – the number of houses their parents owned, the kinds of cars they had arrived in, the name of the schools they had been to. Unlike me they all had been to schools that had names.

My would-be friends went on and I too wanted to listen carefully but my eyes? They became fixed on the most beautiful face they had ever seen! She was seductive, very seductive, like a reflection of the moon. How vividly I remember that first look. I think it was the first stroke of magical Akora!

Her name was Jula.

I am convinced it was love at first sight. I was not listening to how big her house was or how many pets she had, I just kept staring at those intoxicating eyes so much so that I forgot that even I had to speak. But... what could a plain village boy say? I became anxious. What would Jula think? Nowhere to escape, I gathered my nerves and told them about Saviour and its legend, cleverly avoiding any mention of my roots. I was relieved to see that my probable friends listened with interest.

And Jula?

She smiled.

Throughout the day, my eyes followed her like a shadow. I felt like I had known her for ages and she had been sent from the heavens only for me. Oh, how I wished that the day would never end! I wanted to stay in St. Gonava but had to return to tell Saviour what he was missing by staying inside the isolated valley.

The bus slowly crawled towards the waiting mountains. My eyes were not looking out of the window, they were closed to the world and hence could not see that a few strange shadows lurked through the otherwise abandoned rocky beds.

The wanderers of the mela had arrived!

ॐ

People say love is the vehicle in which God commutes; whichever direction it travels in, everything in those surroundings turn beautiful.

I was surprised at myself! How quickly my thoughts had transformed! Just the other day, I had wanted to be at the Market Corner for every moment of my life but now I was ruing over the fact that my classes were not taking place everyday.

I sat in the shop dreaming about Jula, everything appeared so romantic – uncle's sardonic tone, the loud shouts of the hawkers, the honking of buses. Even the never-ceasing blast of the blacksmith's hammer in front of the shop sounded melodic.

Any other day and I would have jumped down from the shop and joined the crowd that had gathered in front of the bakery next door and was being entertained by the huge commotion inside. As she did everyday, the beautiful wife of the baker had come and was bickering about life. She hailed from a big town and had never been happy living in the isolated valley. It was almost a daily routine but today it seemed that the argument had reached ominous levels.

But I was not interested in the least; my mind had taken wings – the thought of getting married to Jula and also shamelessly, inheriting her wealth in the process.

I was so engrossed in my thoughts that I did not notice that a few royal stagecoaches had arrived in our Market Corner and had proceeded towards the jagged road.

I would have continued to be in my world but suddenly I realised that two aged eyes were staring at me.

I had never seen that old, ugly face before. Shabby long robe, heavy iron ornaments hanging on her body and rattling as she moved with a cluster of flies buzzing around her neck, like it was a piece of jaggery!

And that rugged-looking skin bag which she was carrying over her humped back?

Who could have guessed that that ordinary looking bag was full of *pearls*? Not only full of pearls but also in it was hidden the secret of our destinies, the purpose of our existence, the unbelievable reality of our lives!

'Do you want anything?' my uncle who was generally harsh with unwanted idlers loitering around his shop, was surprisingly cautious.

It was only when the old woman had left that he told me about the arrival of the wandering tribe who came from the East, thousands of miles away. He warned me that the travelling clan possessed mysterious powers, passed on to them by their ancestors. I noted his advice of not selling anything on credit to the people of the mela and went back to my world of dreams.

The next morning, as my bus went past the mountains my eyes lit up with surprise. In just one night, the wanderers had transformed the barren rocky beds into a spectacle – colourful ribbons, conical tents, alluring games. It appeared that the news of their arrival had spread fast across the mountains, as even at that early hour people from all surrounding villages had started swarming the mela.

As I peeked into the mela from the moving bus, I could not see much, just a circle of people sitting on the ground like the hawkers of our market, all enticing the crowd, the only difference being the strange things that lay in front of them. The old woman stood near the entrance with that rugged bag resting characteristically on her back and her eyes staring at me.

I quickly turned my head away, as I remembered my uncle's words.

But then, does turning heads turn fortunes? I wish I knew.

*

The next few days were the best days of my young life and remained so for a long time. In St. Gonava, like a bee around a honeycomb, I hung around Jula, always in line of her vision. I came back to my village only to spend time with my future, for it was Jula who came in with every customer in the market shop and it was Jula who accompanied me to Saviour every evening.

I failed to notice that my destiny laughed at me from its vibrant new home, every time my bus went past the mela. And those old eyes? They always stared at me like they already knew what awaited me.

*

My heart was beating faster than ever. During lecture breaks, it was common for students to gather outside the pricey cafés located across our college. For obvious reasons, I had never been close to those expensive doors before. That day I saw Jula sitting unaccompanied under the shadow of a huge statue that stood between two cafés exactly opposite our college. It was my golden chance; to be with her alone, to talk to her alone. I gathered courage and casually walked past the doorman of the nearby café without noticing that out of the two of us he was actually the one better-dressed.

I slowly moved in Jula's direction, pretending to be unaware of her presence, but constantly looking at her through the corner of my eye, as we did in our shops in front of walk-in customers. How beautiful she looked, her deep eyes staring at the statue and her face shining bright in the sunlight! The happy expression on her face convinced me that she knew I was around. I stood beside her waiting with excitement for her to turn her gaze.

I think, young hearts hurt the most when broken...it is a different matter that hearts in general have a desire to stay young forever, a truth that I realised only later in life.

I could have stood there staring at my beautiful Jula forever but instead I got the shock of my life. As the college bell rang, Jula stood up and started walking back but not before throwing an indifferent glance at me! I was stunned to see those unconcerned eyes of hers. I stood frozen and tried pleading with those unresponsive eyes, requesting them to remember. *Mighty mountains? Ever flowing Saviour? A boy always trying to be in them?* I tried to shout, but the eyes just refused, the only thing they said was that they were honest, that they were not pretending to ignore me, they had simply never seen me before. I remained motionless as Jula went past like a stranger but not before her eyes directed me to look at God's vehicle that was quickly changing its direction.

※

The tired bus closed its eyes to rest against the statue, as my heavy feet dragged me down against my will. I was surprised to see the Corner bustling more than ever with life that late in the evening.

The temporary holdings had yet to be dismantled and for the first time the permanent shops did not seem to have any problem with them. Rich shopkeepers or poor hawkers, everyone was laughing together. The discussing groups finally appeared to arrive at a unanimous consensus. A bunch of young children were dancing here and there, drumming empty tins. At first I felt the entire Market Corner was celebrating my humiliation at the hands of Jula. I headed towards my uncle's shop to confirm.

'It is the most fortunate day in centuries for our village... the aged church will come back to its old days of glory... run to your home, your idle father must be happy today,' he shouted from his throne, being as stingy with his words, as he was with his money.

I made my way through the groups of thrilled villagers who voluntarily added links to the curtailed news. The king, whose ancestors had ruled our country for centuries, had set his kind eyes on our village. He had bestowed a large amount of money to renovate the ruined village church but the thing that had made the valley more jubilant than ever was that the king himself was coming to inaugurate the restored church.

It was extraordinary news for our village, the villagers were ecstatic to be the fortunate ones. They knew very well that when a person of his stature travels, prosperity precedes. They knew that the king's arrival would transform the entire village, boost its economy, and change its fortune.

But what was there in it for our family?

My father, now the only roof painter in the village, had got the job of painting the biggest red roof of his life.

Walking slowly in the darkness, I looked at the jagged path; soon it would change, I thought.

I was so used to walking on the pebbled path that I did not like the idea of it being smooth... or of the old church getting restored... or of my father getting the job. It was hard to believe, but that day, even the brightest of things appeared gloomy to my broken heart.

I reached home to find my father scraping the old wooden scaffoldings; the brushes had been clean for ages. With the uncommon smile, his face appeared different yet familiar; it was somewhere there in the faint memories of my childhood. Mother was inside the kitchen, preparing food. But who was hungry? I kept my bag and quietly sneaked out of the door.

I sat silently beside Saviour, under the starless night. Surprisingly, the demon-hurling night appeared far less frightening in front of the vile experience of the morning.

I was quiet and so was Saviour.

I knew it was sad – it was always sad in my sadness.

※

For the past few days Geoga had regularly been coming to the Market Corner pestering me to accompany him to the mela. There was a rumour in the mountains that people of the mela were selling secrets to acquire hidden treasure – something that Geoga had always wanted. All young boys of the valley were warned not to wander near the rocky beds with suggestions that the claims of wanderers were nothing but the enticements of tricksters. There had been instances in the past when a few young boys went missing with their family's earnings as the mela wrapped up and moved. Villagers accused the wanderers of abducting children whereas they maintained that it was the children who ran from the deprived valley in search of a better future.

Whatever the truth, it was enough to keep all of us at bay – but not Geoga. He was keen to talk to the wanderers but was scared to go there alone. I kept refusing; my melancholic heart and tight pockets had little interest in such adventures. But that day was different. . . .

I felt that the fat boy was mad. I did not know which village he came from and what exactly he wanted. And his semi-wrecked pushcart? Who buys from such poor sellers? He had been coming to the Market Corner for the past few days and was offering weird proposals to the shopkeepers: 'Make me a partner, I will double your profit! Send me to the wholesellers and if I manage to get a rebate give me fifty percent of it!' He laughed when my uncle hurled abuses at him. 'You will see, one day I will own this Corner!' he shouted from the footsteps, as my uncle threatened to throw him out of the valley. Disinterested, I glanced at his torn shirt, he smiled and casually headed towards the bakery. What a mad place! I thought with annoyance. The blacksmith's hammer was making the situation even worse.

'Do you ever want to buy anything?' I heard my uncle's irksome yet meek voice. The fateful moment has to come, however much you run! There she was, the old woman, staring at me from the footsteps of our shop. 'A bag of rice,' she said in her coarse voice and handed a dirty note to my uncle without turning her head towards him.

I slowly headed to the back of the shop to execute the order, as my uncle got busy in scrutinising the note.

Nobody knows what relationship words and ears share, some words try for years to enter our ears but are just not allowed in, like the words 'Get out of your tiny hut and sit in the Market Corner for better opportunities' always failed to enter my father's ears. These words even tried to disguise themselves and came from various mouths – my mother's, my uncle's, even the priest's, but my father's ears were clever, they recognised those words every time and forced them back. But some words are not only allowed in but are carried straight to the mind with lightning speed. It does not matter whether these words are good or bad, happy or sad, loud or low, they just have to be liked by the ears.

And as I handed the bag of rice to the old wanderess, her words whispered into my ears, 'Eyes never lie, nor did Jula's... come to the mela... play the game... know the secret of TRUE pearls!' Her words reached my mind like a bolt, as my eyes widened with disbelief. She did not wait for my answer. Her work was done.

༄

'Sleep, my son,' I heard mother's voice coming from the other room. It was the middle of the night. The lamp went out, but my eyes kept staring at the thatch. I had to go to college the next day, but it was obvious that I was not going. I knew that by being absent, I was going to miss important lessons but little did I know that by visiting the mela I would learn what would be the most important lesson of my life.

For the entire night, I slept with open eyes waiting for the sun to rise but as if the moon too was interested in coming along, it just refused to leave. And it was only when my eyes became red that it very reluctantly left, taking the dark sky with it.

Four

~

Humans are strange creatures. Look at animals; a tiger living in one part of the world will be similar to one living in any other part in terms of the home it erects, the enemies it makes, the world it creates. The same holds true for an elephant or for that matter even a sheep. But humans? Humans are strange. Each lives in a world of its own, worlds that are so different from each other that one might wonder whether they all belong to the same species.

It was difficult to leave Uncle's shop early, my half-day shift extended way into the afternoon in spite of my subtle reminders. The sun had almost got over its anger when Geoga and I rushed into the mela to enter a world that we had never seen before.

If seeing one roof was enough to know our village, the mela required at least a thousand visits before it could be fully understood. My shopkeeper uncle would have laughed seeing them doing such weird things for a living. Those strange faces sitting unperturbed on the stony ground – a fat woman with a black snake that helped her search for hidden treasures, a dwarf who could talk to spirits, a child who would remove your future pains by walking on fire balls, all surrounded by a crowd of inquisitive villagers.

The central area of the mela looked a bit familiar with the usual tightrope walkers, sword-swallowers, fire-breathers but then why would one want to earn a living by doing such dangerous stunts when one could easily sell rice?

We kept moving ahead in search of the old woman and had almost reached the end when the strangest, scariest area of the mela revealed itself in front of our eyes – mad looking, half sleepy people, sitting over thorn beds, smoking and singing mystical songs, in between hurling abuses at the onlookers and asking them to leave, abounded. Our eyes tried to look through the clouds of smoke and rested on someone familiar – at the farthest point of the mela on a dark red cloth sat the old wanderess!

We gathered courage and walked past the angry singers and reached the old woman who, surprisingly, had stopped looking at us, as if deliberately ignoring us. I felt strange at her disregard. After all it was she who had called me to the mela. Or did I come because I had to?

We waited impatiently for her to react as my eyes moved around, wondering at the collection of strange items that lay carelessly on her mat. Her display might have been outlandish but unlike the other wanderers of the mela, the old woman was alone and that was odd. Perhaps her tricks were too old to attract anyone.

I became cautious; from my experiences at the Market Corner I knew that an idle man and a busy place was a dangerous combination.

Time, I think, must be the owner of the shop where it works, and must possess a crafty weighing scale otherwise how can it sometimes sell minutes as hours and sometimes hours as minutes?

Watching time converting minutes into hours, my eyes paused at the flies buzzing around her face. Intrigued and somewhat irritated with the sight I imagined myself moving forward and swatting the flies.

Exactly then, the old woman raised her head and gave me a piercing smile.

'Do not worry,' she said it like she had read my mind, 'Soon, you too will want to have these flies hover around your neck. The more of these, the better you will feel!' She laced her sentence with a sardonic smile.

'Where is the treasure?' Geoga interrupted with a slightly raised tone.

'What you do know about Jula?' I added to ensure that we meant business.

'Why invite death?' she instantly replied, throwing a mocking look in our direction.

It had been several years since I began working at the Market Corner and I knew very well how customers get lured in when shopkeepers say, 'We do not show this expensive item to everyone....'

'There are enough sellers in the market,' I said while pulling Geoga and pretending to leave.

'But not one seller like me!' She shouted raising her hands as her bangles rattled. 'And no game...' she bent and picked the skin bag from her mat and swayed it in front of our eyes, 'like the game of True Pearls!'

She continued while lowering herself on the mat, 'But it is not for faint hearts. Especially the coward boys of the mountains who run like terrified mice to their villages before the game even begins. If you think you are brave enough to play then come and sit.' I looked at Geoga. Our eyes met and with some hesitation we lowered ourselves and sat in front of her.

She smiled and heaved a sigh, being slightly melodramatic, 'You boys would not understand. This game is not for everyone to play'.

It was clear that she was an old hand in her tricks – she had our attention and like a skilful puppeteer was now manipulating our strings.

'You think I am lying?' she said with mock seriousness. 'All right, listen to this story and then decide whether you want to play or run back to your valley like mice!' She shrugged her shoulders and started speaking, pretending to be an experienced storyteller:

'Once upon a time, deep inside a dense forest lived a vast colony of small ants. She paused abruptly and threw a useless question, 'You know how these ants are?' 'Wake up ... work ... sleep ... wake up ... work ... sleep. Now, such sincerity should be rewarded. Shouldn't it? Well, so it was! The ants went on working and in the process their mounds kept growing. Soon, those mounds became so big that they started resembling mountains! God is not that unkind, you see!' She gave us a mysterious smile and continued making her voice sound as sweet as possible.

'It was an amazing life – old ants creating mountains and young ants playing in their shadows with pride. Life went on. Everything was fine but one day ... ' she paused narrowing her eyes and looked in the direction of our valley before continuing, ' ... as the ants carried out their duties, a herd of elephants crossed from the front of these mountains. Seeing these elephants, the eyes of one of the young ants lit up with surprise. It was the first time the young ant had seen such a giant animal.

'So mesmerised was it that in spite of the insistence of old and wise ants, it left its game and started following the elephants. The young ant was amazed when it first heard the elephants talking.

The elephants were chatting about a world that the young ant had never seen. Obviously, the young ant was too tiny to be able to see what the giant elephants were capable of seeing. The elephants kept looking beyond the trees and kept talking, fascinating the ant even more.

'Unable to bear its excitement, the young ant finally stopped one of the elephants and requested it to show it the unseen. The elephant laughed and ignored the young ant's request. But the young ant kept insisting until the elephant reluctantly agreed to let the young ant climb on its back and see the world from that height. The young ant climbed and somehow reached the top of the elephant's back. Finding itself at such a height, the ant first gathered itself and then lowered its eyes towards the ground. The moment its eyes reached the ground, the young ant was shocked!

'Their colony of so-called mountains appeared no bigger than a tiny cluster of miniature mounds! And when the young ant raised its eyes? It was spellbound! Spellbound to see the fascinating enormous mountains, the beautiful large rivers, the big bright sky, the wonderful vast gardens.

'Having shown the young ant the world unnoticed by it till now, the elephant finally left.

'The young ant, for a few days, remained the happiest among its group; sometimes even feeling slightly superior to the others, after all, it was the only one who had seen what nobody in its colony could see.

'But a strange thing happened.

'The young ant died within the next fortnight.' The old woman stopped and looked deep into our eyes, 'So, what is the moral of the story?' She moved her sharp nails over our heads and answered herself, 'Do not see what the elephants can see unless you yourself can become an elephant. Otherwise you too will remain unhappy forever and eventually die.'

She leaned closer and whispered, 'Young ants! See the elephants from your mounds, enjoy their stroll, enjoy their eminence...' she paused before finishing, '... Why think of climbing them and become a martyr?'

While Geoga remained firmly seated on his knees, I got up as if somebody had put hot iron rods into the dusty ground under my feet. Her story had pricked my heart like an arrow.

After all, who could tolerate being called an ant?

'How dare she?' My heart screamed. I may have been an ant in the past but not any more. I am now in St. Gonava. Unlike Geoga, I now have a secure future. I am not dying like a failed roof painter. 'No, never! I am not an ant. I am NOT an ant!'

I was amazed at my reaction! I was even shocked to notice that my mind could think of my father in such a derogatory manner. Maybe, the hidden scars of poverty were waiting to come out.

I turned around and had almost started to walk when I felt her nails on my shoulder. 'Be warned!' she screamed. 'This step you are taking thinking that it will lead you to an exciting, fulfilling future is nothing but a foolish thought of a blind ant! Yes, an ant which cannot see its future. Look, young boy.' She pointed towards the radiating horizon. 'Keep looking and I will show you what destiny has in store for you if you take this foot forward. 'Here you enter with your deprived eyes, inside the gates of St. Gonava. See...' she insisted, as if everything was being unveiled right there, next to the setting sun. I tried hard but still could not see anything in the empty red sky. But seeing her tenacity I just fixed my eyes on the horizon, as one by one, her dreadful words started revealing my entire life.

'Here comes the boy of an unnamed village, out of the terrains of an unknown valley. Look, here with his deprived and anxious eyes, he enters the gates of St. Gonava. Isn't he happy seeing the prosperity around him, thinking about his secure future? Look, how happily he is spending his time chasing his rich friends, trying to impress beautiful girls!'

'But...' she suddenly paused, changing the happy expression of her face abruptly. 'What is it?' she asked rhetorically, before throwing spurts of laughter, 'Ha ha ha! Poor boy, he does not know that the people of St. Gonava are cleverer, they are themselves looking to befriend people higher in the chain! Look, they are making fun of him while the stupid boy continues to live in the world of his own.

'What's that? The years are passing by and nothing is happening? Let us see what he does... What *can* he do except replace his pride with flattery! See, he now does nothing in St. Gonava but flatter his classmates in the hope of a decent job.

'Look! It actually works! The boy has managed to convince one such rich classmate to give him a job of a sales manager. The boy is happy. Why not? The salary is good! The posting is in Akora! And the job? An easy one. See, he is making steady progress, so much so that a rich farmer from a nearby village wants him to marry his daughter.

'What else does the boy want? He marries and is soon blessed with two sons. But...' she immediately turned serious, 'Life goes on. The rich father-in-law of his is rich no more as his two brothers-in-law have turned gamblers and are fighting for their father's property in court. But the middle-aged boy does not mind, his job pays enough to afford a comfortable but expensive town life, which he and his family are now used to. But a couple of questions always bother his mind: Why does his deprivation not go? Why does he always fall slightly below the standard in whichever circle he moves – the car he has, the house he lives in, the school where his children study? He gets no definite answers and decides to work harder.

'Time is flying. His two boys are now ready to go to college but, alas, they are not as sharp as him. In spite of studying in good town schools they could not secure scholarships but how can a father see his sons studying at a place that is inferior to where he went? The boy is just about rich enough to afford the expensive fees for both his sons but being a clever person he does not put in his own money. Hmmm, clever boy!' She turned her eyes towards me theatrically and said,

'He borrows it from a bank and sends both of his sons to a college better than St. Gonava, in a town bigger than Akora. What an achievement! The boy is happy again. But not for long.' Her pitch changed again, 'See, as he returns from his work one day, he sees his sons whispering quietly to each other. For a few days he does not hear anything but soon the words become clear. He is surprised! His sons' exposure to the bigger town has made them capable of discussing and scrutinising his life. They think he hasn't done enough; they think he did not take full advantage of his friends at St. Gonava and even the town he settled in is limited in terms of opportunity when compared to the bigger town they are now studying in! Suddenly, the boy sees the same deprivation in his sons' eyes, which was once there in his eyes when he entered the gates of St. Gonava! He becomes quiet, he is a caring father and understands their thoughts, he thinks of migrating but sadly he is not rich enough to afford the same comfortable life in a bigger town. His sons leave, as they are now used to the life in the bigger town, besides, their loans can only be repaid by working in a town bigger than Akora. Time passes, the boy's wife dies, while he grows old. Soon, he too dies, all alone, in Akora, leaving nothing in legacy but his deprived eyes. His sons return to sell his house and soon somebody else starts living in it, in the same way, as somebody else starts working in his place at his office. Hundred more years pass, somebody in his house has been replaced by somebody and that somebody by somebody else; the office where he worked exists no more. Another hundred years pass. Look,' the old woman paused to heave a sigh of relief to show how tedious it was to see my ordinary future, 'I am talking to the eyes of one of your successors, and leave aside the world, he himself does not know that at some point of time, one of his ancestors lived in an unknown valley, next to a stream named Saviour!'

Silence prevailed!

I felt as if I had been struck by lightning! I sat down on the ground as the cursed words hammered my mind. I think that our mind is often akin to a lion. Within its territory it moves and roars like an undisputed king assuring its master that nothing matches its strength. It thrives on conquering weaker brains and enjoys crushing them ruthlessly until the day it finds its match. But being a lion it does not surrender easily, it goes down fighting, arguing and counter arguing, but as soon as it finds its kingship under threat, it submits; and there are those occasions when a bullet or an arrow is enough to bring it down without giving it the slightest chance to fight.

The old woman's future-telling had pierced my mind like an arrow.

Geoga, who had now seen my entire life unveiled in front of his eyes was no less astonished. He hadn't met anyone in his life who had deprecated education, that too with such convincing style. Without charging anything the old woman had given him a weapon, which he could now use to hide his years of failure.

Five

~

The old wanderess had proved her worth. The sun had just risen; people were yet to throng the mela but we were already sitting opposite her with a small stack of notes and coins resting in front of us. We both were now convinced that there was no seller in the mela like her and hence had returned like devoted customers with whatever we could gather in one night. Our empty pockets showed how keen we were to keep her speaking. Geoga now stared at her with mesmerised eyes. He was certain that if anybody could take him to a hidden treasure it had to be her. And I? My lowered head was enough to indicate that my mind had already been captured.

She cleared the stack as quickly as she could and vanished with it into a nearby tent, as we sat there waiting eagerly for her to return. Soon she appeared with the same dirty-looking skin bag that had now become so characteristic of her appearance.

'We have to go very far.' She said throwing the bag on the red mat, 'This money is insufficient for a place like that. The island has the thirst of a hungry cobra.'

We looked at each other in amazement.

'You did not understand even after hearing the story? Do you still want to live in the isolated valley like blind ants? No, boys! The time has come to climb the elephant and see the real world.' She said as her fingers started playing with the rope that tied the skin bag. 'The time has come to play...,' she paused and added with a mysterious smile, 'the Game of True and Dummy Pearls!'

~

'Look carefully, boys!' she said while clutching the tied mouth of the bag as the two childhood friends stared at it with intrigue, 'This bag is no ordinary bag. This bag is full of pearls. Hundreds of them! If you put your hands inside, all the pearls will feel the same. But they are not. Out of them, a few are *true pearls*. Ah! True pearls.' Her eyes sparkled as she continued revealing, 'Pearls that are rare, very rare. Pearls that can blind you with their glitter! Even one would be enough to buy you comfort for a lifetime. But...' seeing us engrossed, she went on, '...these true pearls are not easy to find. They are hidden, hidden deep amidst scores of *dummy pearls*,' she said in a dejected tone while stressing the last two words. 'Boys, these dummy pearls are very misleading. When you touch them, they might feel the same. To inexperienced eyes they might even look the same but these pearls have no value. In the market, they cannot even buy a piece of sweet.'

'Put your hand inside the bag and pull out the pearl of your destiny, that is all this game asks for.' She said and pushed the bag ahead. Her fingers snapped the rope and untied its mouth.

The bag of pearls was now open!

We were both bemused with what she was trying to say and why did she want us to play the game of pearls?

'Do it. Do it!' Seeing our hesitation, she insisted moving her head in sync.

We both paused for a moment before sliding our hands inside the bag of pearls.

As our fingers started exploring the pearls, all of which felt the same, the old woman started chanting what appeared like a hymn from the streets:

> *Sometimes here, sometimes there*
> *Their hands wandered everywhere*
> *But the true pearl escaped all claws*
> *As they did not know where it was*
> *Watch out!*
> *There are loads of dummy pearls with similar wool*
> *And the true ones are only a handful*
> *Dummy pearls!*
> *They are there*
> *So that the bag looks full and large*
> *And he is able to sustain the mirage!*

We explored, trying our best to reach the one elusive true pearl, as the old woman went on chanting in her rough voice, trying to attract passers-by.

Unable to decide, our fingers finally paused. Was it a true pearl?

With hesitation and hope, we pulled our hands out. Suddenly, we felt that everything in the mela had gone quiet; no hymns, no singing, no wanderer, no visitor, not even a whisper.

The pearls of our destiny finally came out of the bag. At first our eyes lit up like lamps but soon disappointment prevailed – the two dummy pearls were even murkier than the pebbles of the Jagged Road in the village.

She laughed as if she already knew the fate of the game and started chanting again:

> *The dummy pearls in the bag,*
> *If reduced are replaced*
> *If increased are picked*
> *They go or they stay*
> *Neither the game is affected*
> *Nor the old woman*
> *Whether they are in this corner*
> *Or that*
> *It doesn't really matter*
> *To anyone*

'Did not understand?' she paused and asked. 'Boys of the mountains, open your eyes. See the truth.' Saying this, she stood, raising her hand and flaunting the bag, its mouth clutched in her fist like a weighing scale, 'Look carefully at this bag. Forget all that you have learnt till now and just remember this,' her voice became louder, as she finally unveiled the mystery of the True and Dummy Pearls:

> 'This earth on which we all live is like my bag. And the people that live on this earth are like the pearls stuffed in it. And like the two kinds of pearls, the people of this world too are of two kinds only. True... or... Dummy. Millions of people inhabit this earth but they are all like the *dummy pearls* in my bag. They live on this earth insignificantly; no one recognises their worthless faces – the faces that all look so similar that they become invisible. No one remembers their names as they keep living nameless lives. All of them merely exist to serve the same purpose as the

dummy pearls do in the bag... just to make the bag look *full and large.*'

As we kept looking at the bag with astonishment, she continued, 'But like my bag, hidden among the scores of dummy pearls this world too has a few, very few true pearls. Wait...,' she paused while her hand crept inside the bag and like a flash came out something seeing which our breath stopped! A pearl dazzled between her two nails like a small sun, like a glowing star! What lustre it had! What shine! Nobody needed to tell us, we knew it could be nothing but a true pearl!

As we remained motionless, mesmerised by its strong glow, the old woman continued, 'Look carefully at this pearl, young boys! Have you ever seen such a shine, such an aura, such a glare before?' The old woman asked, swaying her hand like a snake but our gaze did not break, hypnotised, our eyes followed the shining pearl. Suddenly, Geoga's hand rose and tried seizing the glowing pearl. 'No...no...no ...,' she laughed and immediately withdrew her hand and then moved it back and forth while teasing and tempting him.

She continued, 'My dear boys, true pearls are such people whose fame, wealth and power are beyond comprehension; *fame* that gives them more visibility than thousands of people put together; *wealth* that gives them so much money which even hundreds of shopkeepers of the Market Corner cannot match; *power* that makes them so powerful that they rule millions of people. They maybe known to the world by different names – celebrities, stars, kings, but they mean the same – the true pearls.'

'What is there in a hidden treasure?' she turned towards Geoga and asked.

'Howsoever large it may be, it will only last a few years,' she said and shrugged her shoulders.

'But the treasure of true pearls?' Her eyes now appeared more intoxicated than those of a drunken man, 'It is similar to that endless river of wealth where every time you put your hand in, it gets filled with a new treasure. I have seen them with my own eyes. These very eyes,' she said loudly, pointing towards her eyes, 'they do not walk on earth like you and me.' She said and raised her forefinger towards the sky, 'They travel through air, live in heaven, inside sky-piercing towers!

'Have you ever played the game of snakes-and-ladders?' she paused and asked. 'What happens most of the time in that game is exactly what happens with the perishable lives of all the dummy pearls. Ah! A little success does take them few squares up but their snake-like ordeals constantly bite to pull them down to lower boxes and they eventually die leaving nothing for their kin who, with no support, have to start the game all over again. What difference does it make if you finish at the last, thirteenth or twenty sixth square? You are still far from winning the game. But the true pearls? They reach the top irrespective of the bites and then their life never rests on this stupid game. They get beyond all that... they get chosen!

'They do not look like you and me. No.' She nodded and started looking towards the horizon as though she was seeing a true pearl right there, 'He is wrapped in a glow!' she continued while stretching her hand towards the horizon trying to clutch the air exactly in the same way as Geoga had moved his hands towards the true pearl a minute ago. 'Ah! Every part of his body is radiating! A unique halo is enclosing his face that stands him apart from the thousands of lost, plain faces of dummy pearls that are all looking the same!'

She turned her eyes towards us and asked, 'And how do you recognise that a true pearl is around?' she paused and smiled, 'Flies...,' she said and moved her head while repeating, 'Flies. Like me they also never travel without *flies*! Yes, people like flies; hundreds and hundreds of them, buzzing around the necks of the true pearls.' She pretended to move her neck away from the flies but they followed her like hypnotised entities. She laughed showing her pale teeth and said, 'Look! How they are competing amongst each other to be as close to me as possible!'

She continued while staring deep into our eyes, 'Now remember what I was chanting and you will understand everything. God did not create this earth for dummy pearls. He actually created this game, this bag, this earth for the true pearls. Look at this bag again and think. Think. What keeps this game going? If I say that this bag is only full of true pearls, will anybody have any interest in playing the game of pearls anymore?' 'No,' she answered herself, 'the bag has to be stuffed with the dummy pearls to keep the game interesting. And since the true pearls are only a handful, he needed to create us. Yes, we all just exist to make this game of pearls more intriguing. Otherwise, who will rule a nation where there is no one to be ruled, who will live in a palace where there is no one to gawk at or who will perform in theatres where there is no one to applaud? Dummy pearls die and get replaced. Somebody else takes their place. The game goes on. But the true pearls? They never die. They have conquered invisibility and tricked the inevitable death. Ah! These clever true pearls! They know how to radiate,' she said while moving her fingers over her face, 'How to hook our eyes!

'Have you seen those decorations on the face of a beautiful house... or those patterns on a butterfly wing that compel you to stop and admire them? Yes, in the same way these true pearls distinguish themselves. And how do they defy death? Oh! They have been defying it for centuries by ensuring that the world safeguards their memories. From now on, observe how they carefully get these streets, buildings, plazas named after them. Nothing related to a dummy pearl remains in this world but the true ones make sure that they keep living through names, books, statues – names that last for generations, statues that are as many and as big as towers, books that never let us forget them ... that are dedicated to them – page by page, that tell us all, the streets they walked on, the people they befriended, the places they lived in!'

She paused and turned her attention towards me, 'And ... ,' she stressed on her words, '... under the shadow of one such pearl stood Jula. He was present there only in the form of his statue but this was enough to take your beloved away from you. Imagine what would have happened if the true pearl was present himself?'

'He is coming,' she threw the true pearl back in the bag and repeated with mysticism, 'He is coming!' 'Return! Return to your valley and see what his arrival is doing to your static mountains. The other foolish villagers may not see what your capable eyes can see now. This is the power of this game. From now on your eyes will be open. From now on the world will always appear to you as a bag divided into true and dummy pearls. You will start seeing who are the rulers of this kingdom, the risk takers, the courageous who do not waste their existence and who only exist in this bag like the foam in a glass of tipple.' She smiled and tying the mouth of the bag and throwing it on the ground she spoke her final words, 'Go boys. Welcome the king with your able eyes!'

'Ah! true pearls! true pearls!' Her eyes now beamed with a strange mix of thirst and intoxication. 'How fortunate these boys will be if they carry a destiny like yours.'

Six

~

'No... no... first boulders then red soil, then hard concrete and then soft tar.' One explained the process of building a road while meticulously drawing lines on the ground with a piece of straw.

'What about its thickness and the width?', the second asked in all seriousness.

'What about the wooden bridge?', the third was a reflection of sincerity.

'It will have to be reinforced, otherwise how will that trembling piece of wood support the stagecoaches carrying the king and other royal guests?' the fourth expressed his deep concern.

The discussion went on as my eyes watched them from my uncle's shop while not missing the fleet of trucks that were rolling towards the jagged path. The work which would bring the king to the church had gathered pace. The church was already enclosed with scaffoldings and the jagged path had already been cleared of the adamant bushes; it could now be seen that in the past a path did exist amidst the mysterious forests stretching to the wooden bridge for bringing the outsiders to the church.

The engineers and surveyors sitting in the eatery across had opened up their maps and were busy examining the drawings, hardly noticing the groups of chattering villagers dotted over the open space. But me? The secret of the Market Corner was now out for me and my appreciation for these important gossipmongers had been replaced by revulsion.

I examined their faces as they gathered around like a bunch of crows feeding on the leftovers of others to discuss something to which their contribution was none, arguing over meaningless things. I suddenly felt that their life was nothing else but a senseless argument. I could not differentiate between them and the bulls that wake up everyday to till the earth, the birds that wake up to chirp and fly for food. How could they be so happy, living an identical life every day? I felt like shouting and telling them the truth, 'You are here only to make the bag look *full and large.*'

I raised my eyes and looked towards the rotary, encircling which all lorries and buses rested. This time my eyes were fixed at nothing else but the statue that stood tall inside the rotary. Suddenly something told me that the statue stood there from long before someone even thought of erecting shops there. And that it was not the economics that led the Market Corner to come up here but the presence of this very statue. *The Market Corner or the Statue?* My mind wondered. I did not realise how swiftly the most innocent question of my childhood had been replaced by the cleverest question of my youth.

I was amazed at the power of my open eyes! They were now making me aware of how vastly the symbols of true pearls were spread around us. They had started resting at statues erected inside roundabouts, posters pasted on walls, names written on buildings . . . Why did my eyes not see these before? I was surprised. It was as if these had sprung up in the past few days!

My eyes rose further and became fixed on the mighty mountains standing in the background – the ones that I admired the most. Suddenly I felt that my life was similar to theirs. Being older than me they might have encountered the truth much earlier and ever since must be cursing their motionless destiny which pasted them on an insignificant landscape. Every day they would wake up with the hope that they might be able to move to a place where everybody would notice them, adore them, embrace them. Every moment they would be quibbling and trembling trying to unshackle, but alas! the stationary, ill-fated mountains, they could not move even an inch.

My eyes moved around the Market Corner analysing the rich shopkeepers. The same people who appeared invincible till yesterday had started looking like worthless pearls lying insignificantly in one corner of the world. My uncle whom I admired for his business skills was busy flattering the royal staff in the eatery trying to befriend them. Never had I seen him providing refreshments to someone free of charge. Oh! how he followed them like a tail forgetting that he had a shop to manage.

I saw him returning with a pleased gait and a look in his eyes that showed that he wanted people to know that he was friends with the royalty. I turned my eyes in aversion as I immediately remembered what the old wanderess said about him when Geoga and I complained to her about our poverty-ridden destiny:

> 'Oh! Son of a failed roof painter!' she had turned towards me and said, 'You rue that your father's destiny is not as good as your uncle's? Hear the truth from me now – the only thing that is in your favour is the turbulent destiny you inherited from your father for in its turbulence and

troubles is hidden its urge to see you become a true pearl. Go and tell your father to embrace his destiny because it does not let him settle for smaller pleasures only to push him for higher goals, unlike the vile destiny of your uncle which deliberately does not trouble him to ensure that he remains where he is. Ah...destiny...destiny...if you look back carefully at your life, you will be surprised to find that all major moments of failure when you cried are actually the milestones which shape your destiny for bigger successes and all major moments of achievement when you rejoiced were the devious acts of your destiny which wanted you to slow down...to settle for less. Destiny! What a deceitful veil it wears!'

My gaze slowly turned towards the ground – on the ever-shouting hawkers, the pushcart farmers, the hammering blacksmith. Turbulent destiny. I wished somebody told them.

༄

The invasion had started.

'Watch your side! Not a single scratch on the emperor...the bridge is trembling. Move fast!'

'Careful!'

'On your shoulder!'

The commotion on the wooden bridge became terrible as those burly labourers carried the draped, life-size statue of the king over it and into the churchyard.

Whatever it may have been for the villagers, for me the renovation of the church was similar to the invasion centuries ago. There was mess all around – the rusted iron bell had been removed for recasting, the broken church gate had disappeared. As the porch along with some portions of the church had just been cemented, there was dirt all over the ground.

Thankfully, they had not turned their eyes to Saviour and left the area around it in peace. *Saviour or the church*? The question could trouble me no more!

'Erect it straight, yes there, right in the centre with its face towards the nave!'

Sitting on my rock away from the clamour, I stared at the statue of the king that was supposed to keep him alive! I was surprised that the villagers were not able to notice the intrusion, even when the invaders had managed to enter deep into the church. But could the besiege escape my open eyes? No! I could see that the walls on the inside were now covered with large portraits of the royal family. The benches had been replaced by the newly installed pews, some of which were more beautiful than the others, some had cushioned backs and were closer to the altar. And a special ornate pew was added right at the front for the king... maybe to make him more visible in *His* eyes too?

While watching the ordinary pearls unknowingly erasing their own reminiscences and replacing them with symbols of true pearls, I thought about Geoga. He had gone missing the day we came back from the mela. But this time I knew where he was. He had been visiting all the shops spread over nearby villages where his father supplied goods. It was not that he had suddenly become sincere. In fact he was now on a dangerous mission – dangerous to his father's business as a salesman. Village after village, he had been collecting advances from the purchasers on behalf of his father, lying to them that soon the travelling salesman would return with the required goods. However, he had no intention of handing the money over to his father. He had made all the plans to run away from the valley as if the revelation by the old woman had revived the dying fire in him. He did not know where he would run to but he now knew where he did not want to stay. I was surprised why I was still uncertain about leaving the mountains. Maybe Geoga had nothing to lose and hence, did not care. My mind immediately went to what the old woman had said about the destiny of a destitute.

'We are done with the cleaning. Pass me the paint, boy!' I heard my father's joyful shout from the topmost scaffolding. A large container hung beside him from a thick rope waiting to be filled. My mother, who looked tired due to work, was content with their feat. The long slopes were ready to be painted, as the wild creepers which once looked threatening lay lifeless on the ground. I hurried towards the church to pick up one of the several paint tins stacked on the grass to throw it right into the hands of my father. I had learned this art to perfection over the past years . . . as I had learned to walk blindfolded on the trails of my village. But what was once a matter of pride was now a matter of hatred. Now I was only interested in walking on paths where no one had walked before. I watched as one by one the smaller tins were being emptied into the big container. The church was ready to get painted. Maybe, like me, it was also keen to transform its tarnished destiny. Slowly, the mulish blemishes started giving way to redness.

The sun was at its peak but I remained seated beside the fallen creepers as my father's red brush moved, engulfing every stain and forcing it to blend with the uniform looking canvas. My eyes turned towards the mound of empty tins that lay unattended. Suddenly, I felt as if the paintbrush was like the hand of God and the paint tins like the dummy pearls – the brush had forced every paint-tin to lose its identity and merge into a vast pool of redness. Who could now tell with certainty which tin was used where on the roof? '*If you have seen one, you have seen all,*' the old wanderess had said. I could no longer sit beside those empty tins and decided to run away from them. Was it a sign that I too no longer wanted to live among the unknown faces?

I stood up and unknowingly started walking out of the churchyard; my eyes surveying the activities and my mind wondering, 'The day is not far when a true pearl will enter the unknown valley for the first time ever. However, afterwards the valley will not remain unknown. The world outside will come to know about its existence ... not because hundreds of people have lived here for centuries but because a famous king decided to visit it, what if only for a day.'

As I walked out of the church, I felt a tinge of jealousy against the king. He had never been to the valley but I could see his presence everywhere. I could see his stagecoach galloping on the new bridge that was being constructed parallel to the wooden one at a rapid pace. I could also see the villagers lined up on either side of the jagged road where bulldozers were busy pouring tar. I could also see all the lampposts that were being erected along the newly-laid road, shining bright. The activity was going on only where the king would pass, I thought. Not even a single trail inside the village could dream of getting paved and lit up like this fortunate, once-jagged road which now even had a name.

Yes, a named road in an unnamed valley! And it should not take much effort to guess what that name would have been.

༄

Unobtrusively, on a gloomy wet morning, I got herded along with the unnamed people at the unnamed Market Corner, my unwilling feet somehow boarding the bus with the rest. My eyes remained fixed at the rotary statue, as the queue dragged on. Suddenly the statue looked like a stake, and the bus and we, like the tethered grazing cows. Yes, we were allowed to go to the town but there was a rope around our necks that constantly reminded us that we all had to return. I occupied my seat as my eyes wandered. All these people, willingly or unwillingly, had lent their shoulders to the yoke – incessantly working yet remaining insignificant to the world.

As the bus approached the rocky beds, the old woman's words started coming back to me.

Why was I still going to St. Gonava when I had already seen what would follow? What difference was there between them and me before the mighty king? My heart screamed.

Look at Geoga! I imagined the old woman mocking me. He is the stronger one. He is the one who is not afraid of challenging his destiny.

For the first time in my life I felt inferior to Geoga. Did I not do enough? I immediately curled myself on my seat as if to show that I was not one of the nameless faces travelling along. I was determined that I would not spend the remaining days of my life helplessly under the hoop. To prove my firmness, I decided to abandon my journey and got off at the mela.

For a long time I waited outside its gates and watched the bus turn into a speck and finally get erased from the canvas. The tether was broken and now I waited eagerly for Geoga to return.

Together with him, I too was now keen to know what kind of island it was in front of which even a thirsty cobra would fail.

༄

Words travel through mouths because they hate to remain the same.

'I do not employ kings in my shop,' Uncle was blunt about my regular absences. Which shopkeeper would not be? Especially at such a crucial time. The tale about the renovation of a forgotten church and the reconstruction of a long lost pilgrim road had already turned mythological. *It is the consequence of an age-old prophecy – the church is divine – a dip in Saviour can cure lasting illnesses* ... stories of all kinds were travelling beyond the mountains and changing with every mouth, in return they were attracting a large number of people to our valley everyday. The Market Corner had never been so busy and the shopkeepers were happy with the windfall. As for me, I too was happy; after all it was yet another trick of the deceitful destiny to consolidate their association with the tether.

That day, it was impossible to ignore my uncle's usual tirade. Besides, I had served him enough and the time had come to break the yoke. I grabbed my jacket and jumped towards the stairs, ignoring the baffled customers. My uncle kept shouting from the back, hurling abuses at me.

The words changed again when Uncle vengefully described my daring act to my mother. And mother? I think, every person has two hearts, one in his chest and one in his mother's for it seemed that my mother sensed everything.

We were on the wooden bridge for a long time before she broke the silence with her faint and tired smile, 'All men are like that. Dreamers ... wanting to win the world and ... maybe that's what impresses a woman. Every one of these men has a plan. A scheme that he will cook up all alone – *one strike and I will be out of the misery forever.* What do you think? These villagers ... have they not dreamt? Even your father, he came to this village thinking he would become a rich man by painting all these roofs. His dreams are still the same. These dreamers,' she continued with her eyes fixed at the changing sky, 'you can talk to them about anything but you dare not weigh their dreams on the scale of reality. When these men talk to their wives, they do so with a sense of arrogance... as if the wives do not understand the complexity of winning. You will be surprised to see how many of these men forget to notice their greying hair and wrinkling face. Sadly, for many, their youth fades before their dreams do. When I was young, I was wary of people who left our mountains to settle near the prosperous seas; I was convinced by your father and his dreams. And today, in spite of seeing him fail, as an old mother, I am wary of my son leaving this poor valley. What can one say and what can one do? It is the fate of a woman, and I will have to live with it.' She left with tears in her eyes, I remained on the bridge, tongue-tied, my stony eyes tried desperately to follow her but just remained impassive.

૭

'Heyyy you! Move off the KINGSWAY!' The flies were warned again. The fuming sun returned to the soil leaving the valley under a black umbrella, as I remained alone on the rolling hills. I knew that the darkness was short-lived as it was to be dispelled by a giant necklace that was to sparkle soon. Yes, the unpaved path had finally turned into a smooth, cemented, wide road with a series of beautiful wrought iron lampposts running along both sides making it look like a necklace. And every evening, as soon as the sun went down, the royal workers dutifully lit all the lampposts together to test their durability to ensure that none of them failed on the fast approaching inauguration day.

Tak! Tak! Tak! There they went, one by one like glittering diamonds! And in their light could be seen the barricade that ran along the entire periphery of the newly-laid road almost making it look like an unworn, colossal necklace.

In the past few days I hadn't been anywhere else other than the hills, keenly observing the last phase of the transformation of my village. Besides, where else could I go? The church was too crowded, my connection with the Market Corner was already broken, and St. Gonava? I had given up on my pretence about visiting St. Gonava long back.

I was sure that my mother noticed my regular presence in the valley but my father was too busy enjoying his feat. However, I was surprised at my mother's quietness. Was she not worried? Or did she think that it was a passing phase?

I raised my eyes in the direction of the church – once covered with threatening wild creepers it was now being adorned with a series of colourful bulbs like a newly-wed. Perhaps like a massive pendant hooked to the giant necklace. I lowered my eyes and ran them over the long stretch of tents that had sprouted along the barricade. Everyday, like mushrooms, their number was increasing. And why not? People had been pouring in from surrounding villages to grab the 'closest' view of the mighty true pearl. Leaning against the barricade and staring at the empty necklace, they almost looked like the flies buzzing around the neck of the old woman. The game was interesting. It was like watching pushcart farmers swatting flies that buzzed around their fruits – people trying to jump across the fence and royal guards threatening them with dire consequences. After all, these guards were no longer guarding an unnamed ordinary road. It was now the *Kingsway* and the king reserved every right to be the first to walk on it.

My eyes turned towards the Market Corner and looked anxiously beyond the obstructing mountains in search of Geoga. Never before had I waited with such desperation for him to return.

◈

We entered the crowded mela, but this time with appreciation in our eyes. We could now understand the blithe wanderers a little bit more... the audacious drifters of the bag who managed to run away from mundane life, from the neck-crushing yoke, from the unseen stake. They were free; they were courageous, as they had refused to serve the role of a dummy pearl in the bag!

'To start seeing the yoke is a good sign,' she spoke, welcoming us with a watchful smile. 'But what is the use even if one has open eyes?' she said with a long hollow sigh getting into her typical theatrical mode, 'Many young boys get to this stage but the road ahead is not easy. In fact I will say...' her words froze, her eyes sparkled and her smile widened. She first looked at the stack of notes that Geoga had so confidently taken out from his pockets and thrown in front of her and then turned her gaze to his face with appreciation. 'I knew it!' she spoke with pride, as her hands moved like a magic wand making the notes disappear, 'I knew you boys possessed what it takes to challenge the wicked destiny!'

Geoga had returned only last night. We met each other near the church where, under the light of twinkling stars, he showed me his bulging pockets. His face was brimming with a strange mix of accomplishment and confidence. I reciprocated with admiring eyes – by keeping me on his side, Geoga had proved his friendship.

The words trickled out as soon as the money went into her pocket, 'When with thirst in their eyes and hunger in their hearts men have sailed for thousand of miles from all corners of the world, when several of them have given up on the hope of returning to their homes, when even the harsh destiny gets compelled to give one chance to the few who still have the same fervour in their eyes, then my courageous boys... then your fortunate eyes will set themselves on the mesmerising, fascinating, dazzling *Island of True Pearls*. Such a glittering land, such a splendid land where even the endless sea decides to stop for a moment and stare in awe. And that is the place on this earth my boys where all the true pearls of this world reside. And that is the land where every youth interested in becoming a true pearl has to go.

'The time has come,' she paused and stared deep into our wide eyes. 'Tomorrow evening...' she said in a whisper, '... the valley will receive its king and everyone will be busy making the bag look full and large. Fulfil your desire to see a true pearl and get away from the cursed valley. The ship that takes the aspirers to their dream destination departs in two days.'

My grandmother used to say – something that I never believed – that it often takes the smallest weapon to kill the largest animal, in the same way, it takes the tiniest stroke of time, not years, to change one's life. People like me, who think they are prepared when they face such a moment, realise how weak they are. Who could have guessed, just a few weeks ago, that the valley where I lived for most of my life with my parents and my Saviour would have to be left so suddenly? I remembered the day when I took my first bus to St. Gonava. St. Gonava – my mother's dream! My education for which she had sacrificed every pleasure of hers was now staring at death. No more was I to be 'the first boy from the unknown valley to graduate'. Could I not delay my journey? Could I not do this after finishing my studies? How would I convince my mother to give me permission to leave? As soon as the old woman finished, my mind raised a thousand questions.

As always, the words from the old mouth did not wait, 'A fallback plan is for people who walk backwards hence they all end up where they start. No use in walking ahead unless you burn the bridges behind. Always remember: true pearls are not known by the places where they study – their places of study are known by them. And one's parents?

'Forget asking for permission; do not even think of meeting them before you leave, as who would risk boarding a ship that is destined to enter a storm? It is like this: you are on the ship and they ... they are fixed to the coast. For them to be with you, it is you who will have to anchor. They will never understand you. Never! For he, who has never sailed through storms, can never trust sailors of such ships.' Saying this, the old wanderess got up and so did Geoga. I remained seated as my eyes turned in the direction of the misty mountains.

If my heart had any doubts left, they all got scorched with those very last words, 'Do not bother about your parents, my boy. They will always have money to survive the way they are surviving now. And always remember – nobody dies of hunger ... people die due to lack of hunger!'

Those harsh words echoed through those unnamed mountains for many, many years.

Seven

~

Ting... ting... ting... come... come... come... the only bell in the yellow valley is calling everyone!

The bejewelled old church looked blissful, adorned with thousands of decorative lanterns that dangled on its clean long walls and the bright red roof.

Kingsway – the untrodden path had come alive with thousands of flies – buzzing obsessively around the lampposts in the Market Corner, on the rolling hills climbing up and down. Flies of the higher order—shopkeepers, landlords, rich farmers—were all gathered inside the heavily guarded gate of the church. And surrounded by them, facing the nave, the statue of the true pearl stood tall waiting to be unveiled.

Compline had just ended and everyone in the red carpeted church yard waited, with all eyes staring towards the newly-built bridge. The king would arrive anytime now.

As dusk settled over the valley, the recast crown of the once rusted bell started shining with delight. The festive gongs became louder and louder, thumping the grey heights as if they were a cue for God to finally glance down!

And at that very moment, storming the cloudy mountains, a fleet of carriages galloped into the Market Corner amidst thunderous uproar!

It disappeared as soon as it arrived but this was sufficient for the waiting shopkeepers to applaud as they could now tell their grandchildren that they had once seen the famous king with their own eyes.

'Yes son, the king himself!' They would say, 'Yes! Yes! I saw him with these very eyes. I was right here, on these very steps of our shop. What an unforgettable sight it was! Fourteen white horses drawing a golden stagecoach studded with precious jewels!'

The illuminated virgin Kingsway welcomed its benefactor with open arms. The hills avalanched with people, as the golden stagecoach rolled on the black glass and appeared like a diamond. No! Like a ball of fire and hundreds of villagers chasing it like the sparks emanating out of it. As the horses roared, passing over the new bridge over Saviour, the valley vibrated, maybe out of anger or maybe out of happiness, as now no barrier stood to avoid any further invasion.

The storm stopped only once it entered the newly erected gate leaving the sparks out. The white nostrils flared, the heavy boots thumped, the rifles saluted, as every eyelid situated inside the quad refused to bat. Surrounded by swords, the golden stagecoach appeared like a diamond box holding the most precious stone! Geoga and I stood with our eyes fixed on the carriage along with other village boys on the newly erected compound wall.

The bishop moved forward, the door opened, the bells were ringing continuously, the choir burst into 'Hallelujah' as out came the famous king!

The old wanderess was right!

No face that I had seen in the past had such glory written all over it! It did not matter in the least that the king was old; the aura around him was incomparable – the shopkeepers, the rich landlords, everyone had become invisible in the glow that enveloped the famous king!

The king glanced at his statue and moved towards the renovated steps; the others followed rapidly. We, too, jumped from the wall and rushed towards the nave.

Aides escorted him to every corner that was cleaned by my mother and painted by my father. But where were my parents? Lost in that crowd, nowhere to be seen! Ah! The two most important people in the recent life of the church had now become strangers to it.

The king moved towards the altar scrutinising every portrait, but suddenly his feet halted, he whispered into one of his aides' ear who gestured everyone to stop as the king moved ahead all alone. He did not wait under the shadow of the altar for long. Strangely, he did not even care to sit down on the pew that was solely meant for him; he just turned his back and rushed towards the exit.

As the crowd followed, I silently sneaked towards Saviour; I knew I was short of time. Once the unveiling ceremony finished and the king left, nothing could keep the villagers behind the barricades.

I stood on my rock with folded hands and looked at Saviour waiting for it to react. Saviour was at rest; neither angry nor sad. And then for the first time my heart felt that it was nothing but just a stream – a simple water body stuck between two beds and not a line drawn by God. Realising the truth, my heart ached and tears rolled down my cheeks. I ran towards the bridge as it became difficult to say whether there was more water in my eyes or in the flow beneath.

Scampering on the dark and deserted trails, I reached my empty hut and with wet eyes rushed in to pick up my luggage. In any case, Geoga and I had to beat the king in reaching the borders of the village. But there was one last task that I had to perform. Before I could join Geoga near the barren rocky beds, I had to enter my Uncle's closed shop one last time. Geoga had played his part and it was now my turn to satisfy the hunger of the Island.

As I packed the last of my things, I caught sight of a stack of notes that in the process had fallen on the floor.

It was my mother's lifetime savings!

Did she leave it there on purpose? Did she know that I would flee? Did she know that I would need to steal money? I am sure she did, my heart ached.

I felt a strong urge to see her but quickly remembered what the old woman had said about the sailing ships. With trembling fingers I put the money in my bag, and rushed out of the hut but not before promising it and the valley that I would soon return with enough money to buy every red roof in the village.

༄

And so the boy of Saviour and his childhood friend left for the magical Island of True Pearls. They moved rapidly like two bulls, who had just thrown their yoke away – one with every penny of his mother's savings and the other, with every inch of his father's fortune, looking undeterred and determined to eliminate the invisibility that had marred their families for centuries.

Whether they would become true pearls and shine for generations or whether they would die an unknown and untimely death was something that was hidden in the womb of time.

Eight

~

The uninterrupted whistling of the hesitant train woke me up. Who says dreams are powerful? Always repressed while showing the unattainable, they keep reminding one that they aren't for real.

I saw myself running slowly on the shoulders of the mighty mountains, piercing the floating clouds with a flute held between my fingers, smiling and teasing the sheep that were following me. 'Come on, run faster, catch me... catch me!' I was dreaming and subconsciously I knew I was, as it had always been impossible for me or the sluggish flock to conquer the huge mountains. Besides, by now, Geoga and I were supposed to be on a train that was taking us hundreds of miles away from our tiny red-roofed village.

I drew the curtain from the window to encounter one of the most captivating sights. Having passed through many jungles and many rivers it appeared as if our train had reached the last corner of the earth. An enormous sea stretched as far as our eyes could see; its green cheeks turned crimson in anticipation of its nuptials with the setting sun.

The train stood on the railway tracks running parallel to the vast shore waiting to enter its last station.

The time has come to leave the land of my birth, I thought as I stared at what appeared to be a sleepy town that extended well into the sea. *'Never live your entire life under the same tree,'* my mind was duly reminded of the old wanderess' final advice.

I peeped out of the window and looked towards the two-track railway station and then turned my gaze towards the horizon. The iron wheels came to life and the train moved taking the sun along with it. I envied the train for having such a powerful yet loyal friend, which stopped and moved exactly in sync with it. I turned my gaze towards Geoga who was still in a deep sleep. I was not far behind the train in terms of having a great friend. The last few days had brought me closer to Geoga. I had begun to like the very same qualities that I was wary of in the past – unpredictability, risk-taking attitude, offhandedness. He had proven his loyalty by making sure that we left the valley together.

Leisurely, the train entered its last stop, and I realised, so did the tracks. My feet moved towards Geoga to wake him up. His strong shoulders were much required for me to step out of my small well and enter the infinite ocean.

༄

The sun was just about to rise but it was not difficult to recognise the ship that was travelling towards the magical island out of the whistling lot. While all the ships had thin lines of passengers moving like an army of slow ants, one ship standing tall in the small harbour had hundreds of young boys and girls competing with each other to be the first to climb its wooden stairs. Geoga and I too tried our best to outdo others to advance.

Scampering ahead with my baggage firmly clutched on my shoulders, I looked at those excited faces which had already reached the deck and were shouting with joy, challenging the ones still on the stairs. Suddenly my eyes stopped at two familiar figures which had now climbed the front railing of the ship and were shouting and screaming. My eyes opened wide with amazement. One of them was the baker's beautiful wife and the other was the crazy fat boy who used to advertise weird offers to the shopkeepers of the Market Corner! Never in my entire life had I seen the baker's wife so happy! Like us, she too had bravely absconded from the poor valley, releasing herself from the clutches of misery to pursue what she always wanted – to be visible to the entire world.

I hastened my pace.

Standing on the deck, amidst scores of challengers of destiny, I looked at my land for the last time. The ship whistled, indicating the fishes to give way. Slowly the ship pulled away, the land seemed to slip away from my hands. It seemed angry . . . angry that I and several others who were born on it were abandoning it like an unwanted old father. . . .

I was excited, yet a little sad. Did it have to happen like this? So unexpectedly? So rapidly?

'Of course,' the old woman of the mela would have said. 'It is only in the life of true pearls that he loads twists and turns, the life of a dummy pearl is as straight and as droning as watching a stick than a dancing snake.' She would not have waited for a second to reply.

༺

For days the ship sailed deep into the sea, heading towards the Island completely at the mercy of the incessant sea. At first, the ocean seemed unfriendly, overwhelming, tossing the tiny ship with its huge waves, as though indirectly threatening its passengers to return. But then it also knew that it was not an easy task to frighten away the ambitious eyes. I liked the sound of the whistling ship and the strong sea breeze. Sitting in one corner of the moving deck, I would often stare for hours at the curling waves and wonder if this was my new Saviour? The sheer vastness of the sea seemed to measure up to the vastness of my dreams. Soon, the water started changing its colour and the wind brought with it a unique fragrance. I sensed that we were close now.

And then one morning, I awoke to a thunderous sound, as if something had struck our ship.

PART 2

Nine

There was chaos on the deck. Everybody was running fanatically to the front of the deck which was now crammed with screaming passengers. Hearing splashing sounds and seeing a few jump into the water, I almost concluded that our ship was headed for a tragic end. I rushed towards the railings through the stubborn crowd and lowered my eyes to the water. I was surprised to see that everything was normal but then I caught sight of the skyline and I staggered with astonishment.

The Island of True Pearls!

Wonderstruck, I had reached beside Geoga who stood like a lifeless statue staring at the incredible sight.

The magical island of True Pearls appeared like a fearsome large snake resting all alone in the midst of vast seas! In its north the island widened and rose like an open hood of a cobra to form a huge mountain; for its remaining part the cobra lay straight but curved at the end to form a crooked tail.

However, nobody on the desk was interested in the remaining part of the island as all eyes were fixed on the mesmerising open hood that stood full of pride. I had lived my entire life in the mountains but had never imagined what would happen if men captured the barren peaks.

Geoga had often told me that cobras were considered to be protectors of hidden treasure. To put it simply, no pot of gold could be found without first encountering one of these fearsome reptiles. But this sleeping cobra with a perfectly carved out hood would have beaten any counterpart hands down when compared on wealth. Screaming loudest about its richness was a wide golden streak which ran through the centre of the hood-shaped mountain.

I also remember that Geoga had once spent many months in a forest searching fruitlessly for an extremely rare kind of cobra that is said to carry a precious jewel embedded in its hood. Geoga's hypnotised eyes now clearly suggested that at last his search was over. Unbelievable as it may sound, the open hood had a scarlet coloured, gigantic, sparkling gemstone engraved in its top almost spanning its diameter! The outer walls of the gem were radiating like a glittering diamond with the falling sunrays. A thick blanket of clouds covered the gem on top, like a lid out of which numerous cotton-ball-pieces were oozing and floating, encircling the hood and enhancing its mysticism.

And dotting the skyline, playing hide and seek with the clouds, could be seen hundreds of huge balloons hovering around the dazzling, colossal jewel, each carrying a group of youngsters all screaming with joy.

'That is Jewel Hill . . . heaven on this earth . . . ' someone behind me said. I turned around to come face to face with the baker's wife. She continued, ' . . . where, hidden from the trivial world, live all the *true pearls*. The best of the best. That is the place where a person like me needs to live!' She said and rushed back to pick up her luggage.

The ship was still some distance away from the harbour, but this in no way could prevent some of the passengers who had jumped into the water in order to be the first ones to reach the Jewel Hill.

Such was the lure of the Island of True Pearls!

As soon as the ship hit the island, out came the remaining passengers scurrying down the wooden planks and rushing towards a wide boulevard that seemed like the only major road of the island stretching from the open hood to the crooked tail. Not a single passenger turned towards the crooked tail. Instead, they all ran towards the glittering gemstone.

Before catching up with the rest, I halted while turning my head in the opposite direction – nothing could be seen except the desolate boulevard making a blind turn – it seemed that the curve of the tail hid it from the remaining island and the remaining island from it. Although intrigued to know what existed in the crooked tail, I too did what everyone else was doing.

We ran, screaming and scampering, to the destination of our dreams, which was now so close. We ran outdoing each other, forgetting the pains we went through to reach the island, our minds set on the lavishness of life inside the dazzling Jewel Hill. We ran, putting our unremarkable past behind on the wide boulevard – the path to our destiny, which at times felt weird – it seemed as if it was hollow from beneath and that something moved furiously underneath making me almost believe that the snake was alive!

Soon, we found ourselves standing in front of a short but dark tunnel. One by one we all slipped into it, without realising what unbelievable things waited for us on the other side.

Coming out of the tunnel, our feet halted unexpectedly. The glittery jewel and the shining golden streak were still far, but encountering the nearby spectacle the expressions on our faces changed dramatically, as if somebody had snatched hope and joy out of our eyes and replaced them with bafflement.

Right in front of us, the boulevard had ended abruptly, bifurcating into three huge open gates, each bearing a unique signboard – *Money. Power. Fame.* And as if the entire world had gathered there, each of these gates was crowded with swarms of young people all queued up, and it appeared that they had not been waiting for hours but for days to enter into them.

While Geoga and I stood perplexed, the baker's wife could be seen standing without any confusion in front of the *FameGate*; the Fat Boy had cleverly made his way through the clamour and had already mingled with the crowd standing in front of the gate bearing the *Money* sign.

Seeing the unending queues, the remaining co-passengers had progressed towards the number of posh looking eatery shops which were present just across the three gates.

I turned my gaze to look around. Something caught my attention; crowding the entrance to the eateries, a number of people sat on the ground looking like the street sellers of the Market Corner or the wanderers of the mela trying their best to lure the crowd.

It had been a long and tiresome journey and the smell of delicious food had enhanced our hunger. With some hesitation our feet too turned towards the eating shops.

We had barely covered any distance when a street vendor suddenly jumped from his mat to hold my leg!

'Very strong!' He spoke loudly while examining my calf muscles like a doctor, 'Never have I seen such strength... perfect for football ... come, sit, True Pearl. My rates in the whole island are the cheapest....'

'Old flint!' Before he could even finish, the person sitting next to him intervened, 'Look at his forehead! He is not the playing type. Perfect for the *PowerGate!* Come to me True Pearls. Do not be fooled by this scam.' He warned while continuing to stare at the other vendor.

We were trying our best to decipher what was happening when a baritone voice struck our ears as if it were coming straight out of a movie screen – 'Do not be afraid. They are harmless – the vendors of wisdom.'

We turned our heads. Just behind us, stood a well-dressed, middle-aged man , looking intensely inside one of the restaurants. His hands were empty and he was standing there all alone yet he seemed to be one of those men seeing whom you can immediately conclude that they are the busy kinds.

'How long does it take from here to reach Jewel Hill?' We moved slightly away from the street vendors, towards him, as Geoga posed a question.

'Who knows? Sometimes a few months. Sometimes a few years. Sometimes you may never enter at all.' He answered without turning his head while continuing to look into the restaurant. Apart from looking busy and well-dressed, he appeared to be well aware of life, as his face yielded the right kind of expressions.

'Do you ...' he turned his head and continued, but even before the well-dressed man could finish his sentence, one of the vendors from the street shouted, 'Do you boys even know which gate to enter? Do not waste your time. Come here, I will tell you everything ... which gate to choose....' He finished his sentence in a haste and started untying a bundle that lay in front of him.

The Well-Dressed Man stared at him with raised eyebrows; it seemed he wanted to utter some harsh words but decided to refrain. Perhaps, he was not the type who liked entering street fights. With slow steps, he moved even further away from the vendors of wisdom and gestured us to come along. We quickly followed, leaving the scowling vendors behind.

Standing on the footsteps of one of the restaurants, he waited for a while before taking out an old looking smoking pipe from the pocket of his jacket and taking a long puff. '*Money, Power and Fame* – the only three ladders using which you can climb upto Jewel Hill. Jewel Hill, where only the true pearls live... or their servants.'

He first pointed his pipe towards the three gates and then stretched his arm towards the open hood shining in their backdrop and continued, 'The *MoneyGate* is where the youngsters live and learn how to be the richest. The *PowerGate* is where they all aspire to be the most powerful and the *FameGate* is where they dream and get trained to be famous.'

He stopped and continuing to drag on his pipe in his characteristic unhurried manner, without moving.

'The vendors of wisdom help youngsters in deciding which gate to choose. No doubt they are useful, but it is a waste of money to talk to them without first making a visit to all the three gates.' He spoke with all seriousness.

'But then it could be disastrous to enter these gates without an experienced companion.' He said after a long pause, 'I can accompany you without charging anything, but just to teach you that wisdom sold for free has no value, I will have to.' He added, 'You will need to buy me meals for a week if not more, as I know pockets of dreamers are always tight.'

True Dummy 79

The Well-Dressed Man had made his intentions clear but that did not perturb me. The Market Corner had taught me to prefer shopkeepers who clearly state the price of their goods in the beginning than those who cleverly disguise it by breaking it into smaller parts. I knew charges of the former ones were exorbitant but so was the chance of good quality and prompt delivery.

Geoga and I quickly looked into each other's eyes before nodding our heads in unison.

He nodded in return and spoke nonchalantly, 'We will meet exactly here in one hour, meanwhile, the only thing you need to do is to find a room in one of the inns situated above these restaurants, but make sure that you only take it for the next seven days.'

'And . . . ' He added while walking away casually, 'DO NOT go near Jewel Hill until *I* tell you to.'

The Well-Dressed Man left. Soon enough, we managed to find a room and returned to the same place, waiting keenly for him to explain what the circus in the Island of True Pearls was all about?

❧

In a posh restaurant overlooking the three important gates sat the three of us. I, slightly edgy, turned in my seat and looked helplessly at the Well-Dressed Man who seemed all too engrossed in reading the menu.

Our fears came true the moment he spelt out his expensive order . . . each word of his struck a fatal blow to our resisting pockets. I sighed and looked at Geoga with slanted eyes and then at the Well-Dressed Man, in anticipation for him to start speaking but his eyes had already turned towards the gates.

Food did what my face could not. His attention was back the moment there was food on the table but only to help him fill his plate.

Noticing that both of us were staring, he stared back and spoke those few words, 'In this hungry world, one should never refuse the food on the table. Who knows when you get the opportunity to encounter it again?' he said, as indifferently as ever and started eating. We waited for him to continue but it seemed that he was completely oblivious to our presence; left with no choice, we too reluctantly started filling our stomach... after all, what else is food good for?

As he finished, the words finally came out, 'Let us start with the *MoneyGate*.' He said and stood up, moving towards the exit, 'Perhaps, the most important of them all.'

And the Well-Dressed Man continued over the next seven days.

Ten

～

The *MoneyGate* opened into one of the most splendid places one could ever imagine. Right at the entrance, a few yards from us, was situated what seemed like a large luxurious living-cum-working room with transparent walls, strangely hanging in the air at least ten feet above the ground. The room had everything one could aspire for – a carpeted floor, cushioned sofas, expensive chandeliers, a mahogany coloured working table with beautiful carvings and a kitchen full of food of the best quality.

The back wall of the room was transparent but had become almost opaque due to thousands of currency notes which were glued to it.

The room had a transparent partition and in the other portion there were young boys and girls partying – eating and drinking and dancing in each other's arms while plucking notes from the back wall and throwing them in the air with joy.

We had not noticed, but the room was slowly moving and soon was replaced by another room – an exact replica.

For hours we stood there watching the moving rooms, none of which was vacant, just that the position of the people kept changing – sometimes they were seen lying on the sofa, sometimes working diligently on the table and sometimes partying inside the partitioned portion.

There were a couple of people standing in front of us and when finally, a vacant room came and its transparent door opened, they wasted no time and jumped inside.

Geoga and I were about to follow when the Well-Dressed Man patted our shoulders gesturing us to refrain. Soon, the door shut and the room moved taking its laughing occupants away.

'You wasted our chance to experience that luxurious living,' Geoga who had become annoyed with the Well-Dressed Man's act, was fuming, 'We will now have to wait for hours before we can see another vacant room.'

The Man did not answer; he just signalled with his eyes to follow him into what seemed like a very narrow lane, almost a burrow, situated just beside the entrance taking us inside the *MoneyGate*.

We kept moving, crossing lane after lane, following the instructions of the Well-Dressed Man not to look back.

Soon, we were in front of a very large open ground where strangely a large number of people were squatted like roasters and were busy playing with marbles; the rooms, I guessed, must have been left far behind.

As we made our way through them, I heard somebody furiously shouting while looking behind us,

'Thirty percent profit per year is sufficient?' the man from the grounds screamed while rolling marbles in his palms, 'Fools! I cannot understand what they learn in college. Ten times... you should increase your wealth by at least ten times in every three years.'

'These idiots say...' He turned to his co-player, his arms stretched pointing somewhere behind us, '... sell what the customers want. They do not know that the trick is always to sell to the customers what YOU want and not the other way round!'

Surprised at his ranting, we both immediately turned our heads around and were stunned with what our eyes encountered.

The luxurious room was present where it was, but not alone. It was just one of the hundreds and hundreds of rooms that where all glued together forming an opaque Giant Wheel, reaching such heights that the sky was barely visible!

Almost all rooms of this Giant Wheel were full of people who now from such a distance looked like caged chicken.

'This is the *MoneyGate*,' the Well-Dressed Man finally revealed, 'where everything is translated into money to judge one's shine and hence where everyone wants to be rich. I do not live here and hence do not know what their formula of success is. But whatever it is, I know that their bottom line is, sell – sell earth, sell sky, sell air, sell water, sell nothing but sell. The more you will sell the more the profit will be and the more the profit the more will be your qualification to get inside Jewel Hill. And,' he paused and pointed towards the stuffed rooms, 'That is the 'Giant Wheel' of money makers'.

'Do not make the mistake of thinking that the people working and partying in those rooms are the ones who will be the richest. They are simply educated workers working for their rich masters. Each piece of that Giant Wheel is owned by those playing on the grounds!' He pointed towards the people busy playing with the marbles. 'The youngsters who have jumped into the rooms without realising the complete truth are now so used to the luxury that they are just not ready to come out of that Giant Wheel and walk towards these narrow lanes.'

Amazed at this revelation, I turned my gaze towards the miserly landlords of the *MoneyGate* who themselves preferred to live in narrow lanes but kept their employees in the lavish Giant Wheel. Big or small, they never change, I thought as I remembered shopkeepers of the Market Corner who happily parted with their brand new goods for soiled notes.

Soon the Well-Dressed Man's voice interrupted my thoughts, 'If you can somehow keep educated people working under you, this is the gate where you should stay. However, this is just the beginning. The place gets stranger as you go deep inside. You should see the other gates and know what this Island is all about before deciding which path you eventually choose.' The Well-Dressed Man said and turned towards the exit.

'Stay inside the *MoneyGate*. Nothing can match wealth!' As we all moved from where we came in, we heard one of the landlords shouting to our backs from the streets, 'Once you have money, fame and power can be bought anytime.'

'The last thing one requires to earn money... is money,' the advice kept coming.

ৎ

'Please come in! We have been waiting for you for long. Where is your luggage? Do not worry. My men will take care of it.'

No sooner had we entered the *PowerGate* that this very thin, bald man, dressed in plain white clothes, started welcoming us like he was our long lost friend.

'You must be tired. Where are you boys coming from?' He asked, simultaneously ordering to what seemed like a group of his disciples, who had now moved ahead and started massaging our arms and feet.

'From the yellow valley, the one...' Geoga had barely uttered these few words when the plain dressed man cut him short, 'Oh, yes. I have visited it. What a beautiful place, especially the beautiful yellow flowers and their fragrance! We keep getting a lot of people from yellow valley.' The man spoke with a twinkle in his eye. Although we both knew that he was telling a blatant lie, we did not mind. In fact his hospitality had tempted us to stay inside the *PowerGate*.

'Do not think. Come inside. Unlike other gates here one does not need to do anything. Just eat, drink and live your dreams,' he said, as he held our hands, dragging us along.

We looked at the Well-Dressed Man who nodded in acceptance.

The sight inside *PowerGate* was extremely delightful. Although it was a plain landscape with no construction whatsoever – just mounds of stones, lots of trees and a few thorn beds, it was the people who presented a captivating spectacle.

Oh, the people of the *PowerGate* – some semi-naked, some with long robes, some barefoot, some with long beards, some with not a single strand of hair on their heads, some hanging from the trees, some sleeping on thorn beds, some talking to the stars, some as locaquious as bees and some as quiet as if dead.

But whatever they were, they were all being treated like kings. Someone was feeding them, someone fanning and someone massaging their arms and feet.

'See. Didn't I tell you?' The plain dressed man smiled and answered noticing the changed expression on our faces.

I watched those people, strangely, they all had a big display board next to them on which a random number was written.

'I think I will stay here.' Geoga, who now appeared happy, addressed the Well-Dressed Man, 'With no work and so many people at your service, the path to achieve power seems to be an easy one.'

'Yes. Why not?' the Well-Dressed Man replied, 'Just that you will have to start as the ones serving and not those who are being served. And if you are good at making disciples you surely have a good future here and a much sooner entry into Jewel Hill.'

'See,' he continued while pointing towards the big board, 'the number written on the board represents the number of disciples each of these leaders have. That number is the most important currency inside this gate.'

He said and moved towards the exit. We quickly followed.

'Money and fame cannot buy power but power can buy both. Rich or famous, they are all at our feet,' the bald man tried to convince us, sounding as pleasant as ever.

We left, promising him to come back. After all, we still had not seen the *FameGate* where the queue waiting to enter was by far the longest.

Eleven

~

It appeared as if we had entered a single-street town made up of not brick and cement, not stone and sand, but mirrors and glitter!

Everything on that only street of the *FameGate*—the two rows of shops, the thin pavements, the few trees, the gigantic stage at the end, the street itself—was built of nothing but mirrors.

Adorned with bright coloured ribbons and a series of flashing light-bulbs, the broad, shining street was swarming with hundreds of young people who were all well dressed like the Well-Dressed Man! In fact, better! Their bodies were draped in sparkling dresses, faces coated with white paint and body festooned with glittering ornaments. All these well-dressed people appeared to be in a hurry, coming from nowhere and getting lost inside the glitzy shops.

However, the most unbelievable of all the elements was a series of dazzling poles that stood erect right in front of the rows of shops like street lamps. But what shook the earth under my feet was what each pole had at the top! Like ghosts hanging from branches, each pole had one young person either singing or dancing on its top.

Amazed by the incredible sight, I looked around. No two people appeared the same on that crowded, noisy street of mirrors but what was alike in them was their association with the mirrors; whether they walked or stood still, they never took their eyes away from themselves.

Attracted by a blend of alluring tunes, Geoga and I had barely moved on the street of mirrors when suddenly the unbelievable happened. A group of well-dressed people came forward and lifted Geoga on their shoulders! As they carried him towards the massive stage situated at the end of the street, the entire crowd went berserk – the girls, lined up on both sides of the procession, screamed with ecstasy; they tried to get as close to him as possible as if he was the most famous person ever. The ones hanging on the poles left what they were doing and started repeating his name in unison. Now one could hear nothing on the street of mirrors but chants of 'Geoga'!

Baffled by this extraordinary sight I rushed behind the procession; the Well-Dressed Man who probably had seen it all before, followed sluggishly.

As though by magic, the moment Geoga was placed at the centre of the stage, his image reflected off every mirror that existed in that street. Wherever my eyes could see, there was nothing but the image of Geoga!

Geoga, who had no clue of what was happening, now sported a big grin and waved to the crowd like a star.

He would have hardly spent a minute or two on the stage when the people who had placed him on the stage took him off and put him back on the ground.

As if his feet had acquired some magical property, the moment they touched the earth the entire area went back to how it was. Gone was his image from all the mirrors, the pole possessors went back to their respective acts and the well-dressed people now walked past him like they had never seen him before!

Geoga stood scratching his head, his face looking bemused, yet he watched the Well-Dressed Man with sparkling eyes, requesting him to divulge the secret that could make him famous on the street of mirrors forever.

'By now you must have known that whether it is money, power or fame, the path to achieve them is not as smooth as it seems at first. The outward flash can tempt you but then never forget the hard work that lies behind.' The Well-Dressed Man spoke in an indifferent tone.

'Therefore see what exists beyond this luring street before you eventually decide,' he said and moved towards the almost hidden lane behind the stage.

I hurried along. Geoga too reluctantly followed.

'What do these shops hidden behind the mirrors sell?' I asked, as we moved leaving the row of mirrors behind.

'They sell items of visibility; items that make you glow, that make you stand out, that make you visible – furry dresses, colourful shoes, expensive watches, exclusive ornaments, exotic headgear and yes ... mirrors,' he said and moved ahead.

The Well-Dressed Man was right again. The rear of the *FameGate* was in complete contrast to its radiating front. The people here did not loiter freely as the ones on the street of mirrors; in fact here they appeared more like manual labourers, though of a slightly different kind.

It was an enormously large place with each corner of it occupied by people practising incessantly – some playing musical instruments, some singing songs, some enacting dialogues from famous films and the rest playing various kinds of sports.

'And if you really think that you have the talent to be an actor or a sportsman or that you can sing or dance or compose, you should choose *FameGate* as your eventual destination,' the Well-Dressed Man spoke, looking at his watch.

'So this is it – the story of the three gates. Learn to be the best here and prove yourselves in the *Rings* to be let into those doors of Jewel Hill!' he said, pointing to the golden streak and turned back.

Rings? We both immediately looked at him with inquisitiveness.

'What *Rings*?' asked Geoga.

'What is the hurry? Nobody returns from the Island of True Pearls without knowing about the *Rings*.' He did not pause and continued with the same flow, 'Have you ever noticed that restaurants always serve their stale dishes first? The lunch time is about to be over. So, let us go,' he said and swiftly moved ahead.

Twelve

~

The Well-Dressed Man was never late and hence when the clock went past the usual time of his arrival, we grew impatient. Today was the seventh and the final day and we were keen to get answers to our remaining questions, especially about the *Rings*. To our relief it was not long before he turned up and occupied his seat carelessly. I knew that he would not speak before finishing his meal and hence placed the order without wasting any time.

As told in an ancient story, there was once a king whose life was held inside a parrot, I felt, the words of our Well-Dressed Man were held inside the delicious food in the same way. He started talking as soon as his tongue touched the food.

'Where are you boys staying?' he asked, as he chewed his food.

Geoga opened his mouth but before he could answer, the Well-Dressed Man cautioned raising his hand, 'No! Do not tell me and do not ask me either. Nobody who wants to challenge the *Rings* tells where he stays or how he earns his living.'

He continued, 'Unlike you, the serious challengers of *Rings* stay far away from these expensive streets. And their rooms have nothing but a large mirror. They use their rooms just to sleep and to be in front of that large mirror to practise endlessly.'

His wisdom did not help us. In fact, it made us angry; it was only because of him that we had taken a room closer to the eateries.

'I know what you are thinking, but there was a reason for my suggestion...' he said, 'If I had not told you to take a room here, you would have taken a room in Crooked Tail as that would have been the cheapest....'

He paused and came closer to whisper, his mouth still full, '... But wherever you stay make sure that you do not stay in the Crooked Tail because that is the place where all the poor people of this Island live. They include the servants of Jewel Hill and also those losers who failed completely in the *Rings*. And you must know that if you stay among failures one day you also become a failure.'

Nobody spoke anything after that. The Well-Dressed Man went back to his favourite act and only raised his head when his plate was polished clean.

Slowly, he left his chair and moved out of the restaurant. Now standing exactly where we had seen him for the first time, he took out his pipe from his pocket and spoke, 'There are two ways that can take you inside Jewel Hill. One exists at its front and the other at its back. Look at the golden streak of the cobra,' he pointed towards the open hood, 'That is known as the Golden Passage.'

I raised my head and looked closely at Jewel Hill and soon realised that the golden streak on the hood was actually the boulevard coiling to the peak, just that its usual black tar had got replaced by bright shiny blocks of pure gold!

'If you ever want to enter Jewel Hill,' the Well-Dressed Man continued with his eyes wandering over the youngsters coming out of the tunnel, 'you would want to do it through the Golden Passage and not through the nameless road situated at the back of Jewel Hill, which only the ones serving the True Pearls of Jewel Hill use.'

'But then,' he carried on, 'on the Golden Passage, only the True Pearls can walk or ... the winners of the *Rings*. I know, hearing this you would immediately run towards the *Rings* to stand in it but that is what I did not want and hence advised you not to go near Jewel Hill.'

For a moment silence prevailed, the Well-Dressed Man got busy filling his pipe. He took a few long puffs and spoke as if looking into a camera, 'The *Rings* do not give more than one chance to their challengers. People take years before they put their first step in the *Rings*. If you enter it now,' he smacked Geoga's jacket to make it puff as well and continued, 'You will have no other place to live in on the Island but the Crooked Tail. Right now, the only harmless way for you boys to be closer to Jewel Hill is to take one of those balloon rides,' he finished by pointing towards the sky. We wanted him to elaborate on that but he just smiled in return and disappeared into the streets as though indicating that he had repaid his cost and that everything would become clear once we saw the *Rings* with our own eyes.

༶

Agreeing with the Well-Dressed Man I will not tell you where we took our room, but if you insist, I can only divulge that just beside the three gates hidden somewhere among countless windows was our window too.

The size of your house decides the breadth of your dream ... and the location, its length, is what I found written on one of the walls as we walked deep inside the lodgings of aspirers carrying our luggage. We had no control over the size but we had made sure that our window opened towards Jewel Hill.

Geoga and I stood at our window gazing at the alluring open hood with amazement. We knew the time had come to embrace Jewel Hill and to know what the *Rings* were all about.

Our feet turned instinctively towards the door.

Thirteen

'Sccccreeeaaammmm!!!'

I think people who fear death are those who lack imagination – the ones who cannot envisage what heaven looks like. Flying in the sky in that balloon and seeing heaven from such proximity, I wanted to die! Die, so that I could enter the guarded gates of Jewel Hill and be immortal forever! All my remaining doubts about absconding from the valley, leaving a secure future, turning away from my parents were engulfed by the hypnotising open hood.

Our balloon was now soaring almost right above the golden streak and it seemed that the cobra was ready to strike! The Golden Passage was empty but on both of its sides, hundreds of people were lined up behind the now familiar barricades; their combined buzzing sounding like a loud hiss; their heads raised in unison, turned towards the opaque, undistinguishable front gates of the glittering gem.

My eyes turned and stared at the large number of balloons that were hovering on top of the gem; its passengers bent, keenly looking through the blanket of cloud. I knew their efforts would fail, in fact even they knew that nothing could pierce the dense clouded roof, yet it was a ritual for every balloon to take a round above the gigantic jewel. For the youngsters it was the way to show the Island that their dreams were still alive.

While Geoga kept staring at the sparkling gem, my eyes wandered; I was amazed at the almost perfect shape of the Island. It seemed that the mayor of the island was a clever person, as he had allotted the most appropriate land to the who's who – the raised hood rather than the bent tail; and that God too appeared to be on his side otherwise how could a band of coral rocks run only along the periphery of the mountain, encircling it like a necklace of beads, almost shielding it from the splashing ocean whereas the remaining island had no such defence?

Suddenly my gaze was broken by an intense noise coming from underneath; I knew we were right above the *Rings*!

At the foot of Jewel Hill, the Golden Passage changed its colour back to black and divided into two wide roads that ran along the periphery of Jewel Hill almost glued to the band of coral rocks. And right where the Golden Passage fused with the other three roads, almost acting as a roundabout were situated the *Rings*!

Rings, this was the place where every aspirer on the Island, whether coming from the gates of power, money or fame, had to stand and show his worth! Almost as large as a stadium and surrounded by hundreds of people, the *Rings* were the only way through which we dreamers could enter Jewel Hill.

It was a vast rectangular open area further divided into two squares, each enclosed like boxing rings with two separate entrances. A very long queue of aspirers, many of whom were adorned with the strangest of headgears, body accessories, painted faces, could be seen waiting to enter the *Rings*. Some ordinarily dressed people in the queue were holding large gunny bags. I knew these were the people from *MoneyGate* who wanted to show in the *Rings* how much money they had earned; following them were the participants from the *PowerGate* all holding the boards displaying numbers.

I narrowed my eyes and saw the occupants of the *Rings* carrying on with their acts. The way they were standing on both sides was completely different – whereas people stood like a horde of animals on the *left* side of the *Rings*, on the *right* side they stood in order, one after the other. This classification and the way people stood had a reason as both sides of the *Rings* had different meanings and a different purpose and this was what made the *Rings* the most intriguing of all elements on the magical island.

Right at the entrance to the *Rings* a bunch of people could be seen who looked like landlords from ancient times. Each landlord had a group of assistants, who could be seen around the queue, scrutinising the youngsters, very similar to how the purchasers of animals at the Market Corner would look at the horde. As those purchasers would touch hooves, skin, legs of an animal they intended to buy, these assistants too touched people's hair, forehead, shoulders, looked into the gunny bags, read the number on the display board ... to choose their favourite. These assistants then communicated their preferences to the lords who eventually decided which side an aspirer should eventually go to. It was a decision taken in a few seconds and it often decided the destiny of a challenger.

To the *right* side were sent the youngsters who had real potential to become true pearls in their respective fields – lead actors, lead actresses, singers, dancers, sportsmen, businessmen, politicians. To the *left* were sent those who could at best become extras in their respective fields – one of the several standing behind the hero, one of the several singing along with the lead singer, aides of tycoons, sidekicks of world rulers....

As our balloon approached the ground, I heard the sound of a gong. In an instant, the ones standing in the *Rings* started performing – dancing, singing, acting, delivering speeches, showing business skills. This was the time for which some of them had waited for years!

They were not doing all this to please themselves. They knew that their actions were being closely watched. I turned my eyes and looked towards the numerous towers hanging on top of the *Rings*. These were the eyes of the Jewel Hill – cameras attached to the towers beaming images from the *Rings* to the true pearls resting in the heavens – filmmakers looking for the next shining star, wealthy financiers looking to fund business prodigy, club owners in search of the next sports wizard... all sitting in their respective towers inside the Jewel Hill and judging the fate of the next true pearl. And everyone in the Island knew that their eyes would only be focused on the *right* side, as to choose among the extras was not their job. That was left to the landlords standing on the ground.

Soon the gong sounded again and everybody inside the *Rings* stopped as unwound toys. Everything around the *Rings* went silent in anticipation.

After a brief while, the landlords came to the *Rings* and made that ominous announcement – one more round of the *Rings* had gone unfruitful.

It took months for somebody to be chosen from the *Rings*, to walk on the Golden Passage and to be taken inside the glittering world of true pearls.

While the lords got busy instructing their assistants to choose a few among the extras, the occupants of the *right* side left the *Rings* with their heads down making way for the new lot to come in. They had lost their only chance and God only knew what they would be doing after this – start standing on the *left* side? Start performing on the streets? Start living in the Crooked Tail?

My head instinctively turned towards the tail, as our balloon prepared to land. I very well knew by now that if Geoga and I were not to end up there, we had to soon start thinking about how we were challenging the *Rings* – *Power*? *Money*? *Fame*?

My eyes turned towards the entrance of the three gates. Perhaps, the time had come to ask the vendors of wisdom, which of the three gates we should choose to be able to walk into the glittering heaven.

Fourteen

~

'Those bitten by the snake of invisibility are best suited to choose the ladder of *Fame* over *Money* and *Power*!' The tall bearded man spoke with certainty, his face submerged deep down into his almost torn book, as he carefully turned its soiled pages with shivering fingers.

After a lot of unsatisfactory experiences, Geoga had discovered this drunken vendor of wisdom in some obscure corner of the Island. There was a strong rumour that he was once a wealthy and famous actor who actually lived in Jewel Hill but due to his spendthrift lifestyle and excessive drinking, was now reduced to living in the streets, selling wisdom. Looking at his tattered state I could safely say that his chance of ever being a celebrity again were as grim as that of the alluring Island turning into a deserted place.

'Fame, money and power – these three share a strange relationship. Fame brings fame for sure and to clever people it also brings money and power but in smaller derivatives. The same holds for the other two. For example, a person climbing the ladder of wealth may get fame and power but in what proportion, nobody knows,' he said. 'You may choose what you want but I can bet that you both might live happily with little money and

True Dummy 101

power but never without fame.' Geoga and I listened to him with rapt attention.

'How does one become famous?' The words came out of Geoga's mouth instinctively.

'Yes, how does one become famous?' I repeated without wasting any time.

'I study these people everyday when they arrive,' he spoke without answering our question, pointing towards the clusters of youngsters emerging out of the tunnel and queuing up in front of the three gates. 'I study their gaze, their pose and regularly weigh them on the scale of talent, ambition, courage and destiny.. Could that boy,' he pointed towards a particular group standing in front of the *PowerGate* and continued, 'who seems like the leader of his group, be the next ruler of the Island?' 'Or,' he pointed towards another boy holding a pair of shoes in his hands in front of the *FameGate*, 'Could that be the next football hero? Or that girl, who is the most beautiful among her friends, could she be the next successful actress?' He continued, spilling his grand scheme, 'I am working on it and within a few months I will be able to train my eyes to spot a potential celebrity. It is an amazing talent; enough to take me back to Jewel Hill and make me famous again.'

'But returning to your question, how does one become famous? How does . . . ?' he said, staring into oblivion. 'Is one born like that? Is it in one's stars, in a prophecy? Is it about being gifted? I mean some people are just born with it. Nobody knows how but they somehow manage to identify their hidden talent at some stage of their life and eventually become the undisputable kings of their chosen field. But is everyone born with a gift? Or can all this be achieved by hard work, dedication, persistence and a favouring destiny?'

He paused for a while, staring into nothingness but soon shook his head and turned his attention towards us, 'Many people come to the Island and try different things. They spend a few years contemplating about the three gates but never really find out what they're best at – making money, leading people or earning fame? If you can pay me for just one more bottle of wine I will reveal to you my most impressive theory that can help you crack this puzzle.'

His eyes lit up as soon as Geoga nodded and looked towards me. I reluctantly reached into my pocket and pulled out what seemed like the last few coins out of everything that I had brought with me.

The drunkard kept his tattered book cautiously on the ground and lifted both his hands to hold Geoga's head, 'This brain of ours,' he spoke as if he was revealing his best kept secret, 'is actually further divided into two brains, which are like two houses separated by a long wall with a small window. In one house lives a female magician all chained up and in the other house lives her master, a rational male holding one end of the chain. The female magician is the one who is born with a gift, however, she is illiterate. She only knows how to perform. She does not know how she is able to dance, sing or act or play or what the technique behind it is and neither is she interested in acquiring any knowledge about how she does what she does and hence there are no books in her house. The rational male, on the other hand, is the one who is born with the skill to observe and analyse and he is literate. Hence, unlike the empty house of the female magician, his house is full of books. However, unlike the rational male, the female magician does not care about the world. Even though she is chained, she practises her talent for herself, at her own discretion, to make herself happy. She cannot be forced, no matter how strict the master becomes. Hence, whenever she performs, the rational male quickly goes to the small window and quietly observes her, analysing and noting down every move of hers. Once he finishes his observation, he reads all his books and tries to learn the technique himself. If he manages to outperform the female, he hides her and talks to the world himself and if he finds her tricks to be too refined and complex, he lets her talk. The reason why talented people perform exceptionally well is that there is no rational male living in their mind to master the magician. The female is happy and free, but due to the absence of the rational male she is not able to control her interaction with the world and easily gets tricked, making talented people end up in misery and anonymity. Some talented people are very fortunate as they not only have a rational male, but their female magician is madly in love with her rational master. She performs to keep him happy and because of their romance these talented people rule the world. People are sometimes surprised when a talented person suddenly turns into a pale shadow of himself... this is precisely the time when the romance is broken and the rational male performs all alone with all that he can faintly remember,' he paused, as his hands left Geoga's head and ended his discourse, 'Now what you should do is ask your female magician to reveal what her gift is and if she remains silent, ask your rational master to suggest which field you are most likely to succeed in. And always remember, it is their romance which is the most important to make you rise higher and higher,' he leapt towards the coins as he finished his speech.

Fifteen

~

'May I sit here?' someone asked as I felt a warm touch on my shoulder. I turned my head. She stood there overlooking me, her grey hair waving, her eyes sparkling. Although well advanced in age, all efforts of time were turning futile in front of her friendly face.

'I want to see the sun through your eyes,' she said with a childlike smile.

I had been walking aimlessly, lost in my thoughts, and had ended up far away from the three gates. It had been several days since Geoga and I had met the drunkard and with each passing day my misery was increasing – I had still not figured out my gift, the one I was born with. In a way, I had grown into a sixteen-year-old with absolutely nothing. I could not draw landscapes, play musical instruments, write poems or sing songs. Like many, I did a little bit of everything – sports, dancing, acting, painting – sometimes for pleasure and sometimes under pressure, but never with the passion that could win the world. I had spent every minute of the past few days tracing the existence of the female magician in my head, but the result was an absolute zero. The only thing I could conclude was that there had been certain moments in my life, God knows how, when nothing went wrong in some field or another, when I seemed a champion; one flawless movement of the paint brush, a magical goal in an exciting situation, a verse said in perfection, a moment in a school play when the line between reality and acting blurred and so on. But then, those were just moments and most of the time it felt that it was not me in them. They seemed like magical moments, a lucky coincidence. Were they the moments when my female magician was trying to be happy or were they just an act of chance? I could not figure it out.

There was another reason for gloominess – the fast depletion of my mother's savings. The Island truly had the hunger of an unfed cobra where the only way to keep your dreams alive was to have deep pockets. All youngsters had to invariably have a well-paid part-time job to support their struggle. However, finding such a job in this hungry Island was like asking a pushcart farmer for a credit sale in off season. Geoga's travelling experience had come in handy; he had already charmed his way into a salesman's job in one of the *FameGate* shops.

The Market Corner had taught me that a partnership can only survive between partners of equal strength, so now the pressure was really on me to keep pace with my partner.

Sitting on the seashore with the harbour behind me, I had been observing her for the past few days. She could always be seen on the beach with a piano and a group of children sitting in a semi-circle around her. Although they were at a distance and I could not clearly see what they did, something suggested that they were all part of some kind of classroom. Maybe she was a music teacher? I wondered. But then I never saw her play the piano.

We remained silent for a while before she broke the silence, 'It must have been hard to leave your parents without letting them know.'

I turned my head in amazement. 'How did you know?'

'Do not think that I am also one of those vendors of wisdom of the three gates,' she answered immediately. 'I just guessed. It's the story of most of the youngsters who come here. I see you here everyday, I can safely predict that you still have not found a job.'

I was surprised again!

'I am Ira. I teach the children of Crooked Tail,' she said, pointing towards the curved end of the island.

So she was a teacher, I thought but did not speak. Again silence prevailed. We remained seated, our eyes watching the sunset.

'I can get you a job,' Ira said in a casual tone.

I took my eyes off the sun and looked at her, trying to reassure myself that she had really said what my ears had heard.

'The work you need to do is not easy, so listen carefully before you say yes,' she said.

Ira continued after a long pause, as her words started revealing more about her 'It is said that even if you cut the tail of a snake, it does not die. Perhaps, that is why the people on the Island have forgotten that a few people live even beyond that curve.'

'Crooked Tail,' she sighed and continued, 'is a place where two things will never change – poverty and hundreds of young children playing football in every corner. Day or night, rain or sunshine, whenever you walk into the tail you see young boys always playing football on its narrow streets with only one single dream, a dream that someday they all will become famous club players. But it was not always like this.

'Long ago, as the Island was waking up, it heard that a young boy from the poor end of the island had been successful in entering the *Rings* and was playing football like a magician. Word spread and people from all over swarmed to catch a glimpse of him. They watched in astonishment as the barefooted boy played with the ball as if it was glued to his feet! That day, for the first time, the people of the unknown tail saw one of their own riding up to the heaven with a glittering crown. It is said it was the best day in the history of these impoverished people. But for me, it was the worst. It was the day when all their children turned away from school and ran to the open spaces to play.' Ira paused and I wondered what was it that she wanted from me.

Soon it became clear.

'It is good that they dream of becoming stars,' she continued, 'But not everyone can, and eventually education is the only thing that will help them lead a better life. Your work,' she turned her head and looked into my eyes, 'will be to convince these boys to go to school. The more boys you convince, the more commission you receive. And the ones who are absolutely reluctant to come, you will teach them at the location preferred by them. The more people you teach, the more money you get. But . . . ' she paused, '. . . teaching these boys what I want will be difficult unless you have learnt it yourself. And hence, you too will need to spend time in my classroom,' she said, pointing towards the piano standing all alone on the deserted shore.

It appeared that I was listening but actually my ears were somewhere else. They had rebuffed Ira's words and were telling my brain to recollect what the old woman had said about education. I wanted to repeat the harsh old words but refrained. I did not want to jeopardise my only job offer. Besides, it was not my concern whether the education harmed or helped the Crooked Tail boys.

I agreed, but out came the words that summed up my views on the poor end of the Island, 'What would you teach to a place that remains poor in spite of being so close to a sea?'

Ira went silent and stood up to leave. I became apprehensive. Was she angry? I rued my words. Suddenly I heard her laugh.

'What would you teach the wealthy who keep their neighbours poor?' she shouted loudly to the sea before running away from it like an innocent child who runs away after teasing her grandparents.

That was Ira! I still had not been to her class but she had already given me the first lesson.

Sixteen

~

The excitement in our nerves had reached its limits. Our ears stood vigilantly right next to the merciless gong like obedient servants of our brains. Our feet that were frantically changing their position to scrutinise her performance from all angles, were now glued to the ground; our eyes transfixed at that one particular challenger.

For the thousands surrounding the *Rings*, it might have been like any other day but not for the two boys from the yellow valley.

Today the *Rings* were challenged by the Baker's Wife. And what a challenge it was! She had spellbound the crowd with her exemplary acting. A month's stay at the Island had excavated her gift that had been buried inside her in the dark mountains of the valley for years and had let it loose like hot lava flowing from a volcano that had become active suddenly.

People spent years on the Island learning what exactly to pick from the crammed shops of *FameGate* in order to be outstanding. But not so for the Baker's Wife. The day she arrived, she knew exactly what to buy and from where. We often spotted her in ordinary attire wandering around the *FameGate* shops, without realising that she was meticulously buying items and stocking them for the most important day.

With her beguiling appearance and astounding gaze she had captured every assistant's interest, astounded all the lords of the *Rings* and had immediately found her way into the *right side*.

And now she was performing. Her big eyes depicted every emotion that could exist in a human being, her long legs performed in the *Rings* like those of an intoxicated peacock; her body swayed, like a just-ripe spikelet of wheat standing all alone in a field romancing the sensual breeze.

The supercilious Gong sounded! She stopped in an instant and looked towards the hanging towers – it was clear that she was not interested in the earthly lords but only in those living in the heavens.

What happened in the next few minutes remained embedded in our young minds for many months. Those who had gathered around the *Rings* that day were definitely the fortunate ones – witnessing the crowning ceremony of a challenger of the *Rings* was considered to be the most auspicious thing that could happen to the aspirers of the three gates. Once witnessed, it would never let the dreamers sleep, igniting a fire in their chest that could only be doused by an entry to Jewel Hill.

For a moment, it seemed that the sky had burst with anger. But no, it was not the sky, it was the closed gate of the heaven that had opened with a thunderous bang from which a dazzling ball of white light emerged in a flash and was now rapidly rolling down the Golden Passage!

Never in the past had the streak of the cobra rippled with such intensity and such a loud hiss. The barriers almost caved in with the weight of *flies*, as the bright white ball turned into a magnificent chariot drawn by a troop of black horses.

The chariot halted near the *Rings* but only for a few seconds. In a flash, four well-dressed people jumped from its back smiling; apparently these were the servants of Jewel Hill.

The Baker's Wife now stood inside an open palanquin which was carried on the shoulders by the four servants towards the white chariot. She waved at the crowd not as a newborn star but as a veteran for whom it was an everyday affair.

The palanquin stopped near the chariot and waited. The door opened and out came just a hand, ready for the Baker's Wife. As if the appearance of the hand was magical, the entire area started getting showered with rose petals. People burst into hysterical screams, jumping as high as they could to snatch blood-red petals from the air.

Quickly, the hand and the newly crowned true pearl disappeared behind the locked door of the chariot. The horses retreated and galloped towards the gates of heaven.

As the chariot disappeared behind the clouds these words came out from the mouths of two people exactly at the same time, 'Having encountered this sight of glory, how else would one want to leave earth and reach the heaven but as a famous actor!'

No, it was not me and Geoga.

It was me and someone standing right behind us.

We turned our heads to see.

Seventeen

~

It had started raining as I walked through the stained streets of Crooked Tail, a place that I presumed was too laid back, too happy to remain poor. The tail was fortunate or maybe unfortunate to have the sea as its neighbour, as the ones who could not work as servants of Jewel Hill relied on its water to survive. Old or young, they all earned their living through fishing – the enterprising ones caught them, the less enterprising ones sold them and even lesser ones worked happily as labourers for a wealthy merchant who owned almost all the trade in Crooked Tail.

As I walked through the ramshackle buildings, their worn-out walls dotted with posters of football stars, I saw boys half my age playing the game at every corner even in the rain. Barefoot and mud-splattered, their dedication was unmatched by any other yet I doubted their destiny.

Like an agile fisherman, I walked through the narrow streets, constantly looking out for children who I could bait, because by now I had learnt that it would take no less than an expert to bring these children back to schools.

Yes, it was Ira's extraordinary classroom where I had had my initial angling lessons. It was extraordinary, something I had never seen before; a roofless room without a blackboard, without any books, without rows of seats, just she and her piano.

Her explanation for this unusual arrangement?

'I am not a comedian and this is not a theatre. I do not teach through books, the books teach themselves. This is a place where I learn from you and you learn from each other,' she said as she made us sit in a circle around her piano.

And why did she have the piano?

To keep reminding us that education is like creating music. Just as the seven key notes, its principles are also fixed but it too has endless potential to create new melodies all the time. I was surprised by the way the piano appeared to her: not merely as a musical instrument but as a fellow teacher.

> *It is exhausting to play the piano*
> *But the sound produced is pure*
> *My teaching will be successful*
> *If you take its route more*
> *Don't step on any, as it won't win you medals*
> *But if you ever want to, step on its pedals.*
> *Do your ears require oil or your palms need grease?*
> *I wish you all create a world like 'it'*
> *Where the black and the white live together in peace.*

She made sure to mention this everyday.

There were very few students in Ira's classroom and most of them, like me, were there because they had made a commitment to her. But she did not care. Unlike the performers of the three gates, she was more than happy with her small audience.

Ira's classes mainly comprised fables, parables and poems, most of which appeared to be self created. Her requirement, as an employer of us was simple – 'Walk around the streets of Crooked Tail with your pockets full of my stories and poems and do not return before emptying them in front of as many children as you can.'

To me, Ira was a strange trader, selling exactly what I wanted at a cost that I was more than happy to pay. Her condition, that we all attend her classroom compulsorily took me back to that night when my mother and father argued over the milk-less calf. Ira's requirement was similar to the promise my mother took from my father.

I did not tell Geoga about my job as I knew he would get upset about my spending time outside the three gates. But I was happy inside. I knew I would never graduate from St. Gonava, but spending time in Ira's classroom helped in reducing the guilt of shattering my mother's dream.

I kept walking, under the drizzle, watching the busy children, in search of my first catch.

Eighteen

~

'Talent without practice is like a bow that has never been mounted; practice without talent like an arrow fired without a bow.' The man growled like a feisty leopard, strolling on the huge stage which stood in one corner of an open ground somewhere deep inside *FameGate*. He was a short man with a medium built and average looks yet his walk had the credence of a seven-feet-tall fighter who had returned victorious from the battleground. He did not have the attire of a soldier or any weapons in his hands, still to all of us he seemed soldier enough. Just a few minutes ago he had thrown a real sword towards his audience challenging them to come up and fight. But none of us could gather that courage. Yes, in spite of the fact that his hands were empty now.

Such was the magic of his acting. And probably, that is why he was the most revered acting guru of *FameGate* – the one who had sent the most number of challengers to Jewel Hill.

Geoga and I stood surrounding the stage with hundreds of other aspirers taking our first lessons in acting. Witnessing the grand entry of the Baker's Wife into the heaven and spending a few evenings in front of the Show shops were enough to convince us to become nothing else but famous actors – those who could raise the maximum number of barricades and attract the highest number of *flies*.

'Now, before we disperse, let me demonstrate to you the ultimate test in acting.' The guru said and lowered himself on the stage. 'The day you will pass this you can assume that you are prepared to challenge the *Rings*. No more will you need to come back to learn how to act.' His eyes closed.

To our utter amazement, in no time his body started swaying as if some kind of imaginary force wanted to throw it off the stage. His fingers strongly gripped the floor in resistance, as he started sweating profusely.

'You cannot see but the power of acting has made me travel thousands of miles and flown me right into a forlorn desert!' He shouted and his voice echoed as if he was really standing in the middle of nowhere.

'Oh!' he covered his face with his palms and shouted in a choked voice, 'The strong wind is forcing the sand into my eyes.'

'Look!' Suddenly he screamed with elation, 'I am standing right next to the beautiful pyramids!' he rolled his eyes in admiration as if a huge pyramid stood right next to him and continued –

'I am here not because I want to see or touch a pyramid but to talk... to extract the secret of success from its stones which have been resting one above the other in layers for centuries.' He spoke with full force and moved his ears closer to the imaginary pyramid. The closer he went the redder his face became. Soon a smile appeared on his face as if he had convinced the pyramids to talk.

In a flash his eyes opened as a stunned silence prevailed.

The test had ended, he had passed with flying colours.

He stood up and spoke while wiping his sweat off, 'You all will be perfect actors the day you can see a pyramid at your own will and manage to convince it to let its secret out. Try now. Let us see how many of you can achieve this feat?'

Like others, I shut my eyes and tried.

Leave aside seeing pyramids; I was not even able to keep my ears away from the distracting noises that were coming from all corners of the *FameGate*. I opened my eyes in frustration.

The stage was empty, the guru was gone.

We knew it was time to disperse.

'Oh, risk takers!' It appeared as if the melodious words came out of a honey pot. We were about to leave the practice ground when we heard that captivating voice. Our heads turned as my heart skipped a beat again. She was the same girl who stood right behind us on the day of the crowning in the *Rings*. That day we only had the opportunity to exchange smiles.

I am sure if my heart could, it would have turned into a stone the moment I set my eyes on her and also would have enticed my breath to do the same so that I could gaze at her forever. Her face appeared like it had been carved by the finest sculptor. Her pink lips could be easily mistaken for rose petals, her eyes for a deep blue ocean. Her skin glittered with a unique golden yellow tinge and her silver gown made it appear like she was surrounded by floating clouds.

'My name is Verona.' She introduced herself with a hypnotising smile while her hands slowly caressed her shoulder-length, golden curls. 'We have a long battle ahead...,' she spoke with immense confidence and poise, '...and the weather of the Island is fickle. Hence, it is always safe to be under the shadow of friends.' She completed her sentence and extended her arm.

It was only a few days ago that I had got a decent job.

A smile ran over my lips. Happiness or sadness, I guess God likes to give in pairs.

We shook hands automatically.

Nineteen

~

The overflowing sea appeared to engulf everything in its vicinity.

I feared getting closer, appearing somewhat sad and remembering the gentle Saviour whose waves were always indirect and encouraging in their answers.

'Can there be a scabbard with more than one sword?' I asked the stormy waters.

'Yes. Only if you can show me a kingdom with more than one king,' taunted the sea.

I found myself asking strange questions from the stormy sea which unlike Saviour was upfront. Perhaps, the constant downpour from the skies over the past few days had turned it violent.

It had been more than six months since we started our struggle in the Island. The good part was that we were managing well in continuing to feed the hungry cobra. Ira turned out to be a generous employer. Although I did my job with sincerity, my success rate was not great. Bringing those dreamers back to school was something I found extremely difficult. How could I teach them something in which I myself had lost faith? Come back to school! Why and what for? *Of course to become learned slaves in the fish-based economy still required to serve the wealthy merchant!* What's more, it seemed that the entire Crooked Tail was intoxicated with the *true pearl dream* as though the old woman from the mela had been visiting them for generations. Make them sleep on streets, keep them hungry or throw them in the sea, they were happy as long as they could hope to enter Jewel Hill just once.

And who could sell earthly things to these mad devotees of heaven?

Whether it be the streets, market or sea, wherever I tried, '*Go away! Schools do not teach how to become a star*' was the statement I always returned with. However, in spite of my little success Ira kept investing in me.

Geoga was also earning well; just that, unlike me, his employer changed every month. His relationships with them were never better than the one I had with my shopkeeper uncle. To Geoga they all appeared like him – never satisfied. But then who was in need of beautifying a resume? He was the master of his own will. One unbearable comment and out he walked with the 'one day you will see' look in his eyes.

So, it was not our survival that was worrying me but... my performance at the acting academy. No matter what I did, I was not able to make any impression on the guru or my fellow aspirers.

In my early days, I performed with a lot of enthusiasm but with no appreciation for my work from anyone, I was losing confidence. I was now unsure whether I was worthy enough to be an actor. In a few months the guru was to announce names of people who, according to him, were wasting time in pursuing the dream of challenging the *Rings*. I feared the worst.

I could not think any further as I saw Ira walking towards me. I did not know how, but she always found me whenever I needed her, always ready with an answer.

'You haven't heard my famous fable, "A Horse and a Donkey"?' she exclaimed teasingly. She had successfully pestered me to speak about my concern; she always managed. I think nothing interested her more than an opportunity to tell a story or a poem.

'Once upon a time . . . ,' she sat down next to me and started; she always started like this without caring that such opening sentences did not sell anymore, ' . . . there was a horse and there was a donkey running together in a race of horses and donkeys. A point came in the race when they found themselves running side by side. For a few days, they both ran quietly, ignoring each other's presence, but one day the horse heard something, which he hadn't heard in his entire life! Unbelievable as it sounded, he tried to listen carefully to what the donkey was repeating, "It is not me, it is you who is a donkey."

'At first, the horse kept running, unruffled by the statement but as the donkey kept repeating it again and again in its loud bray, doubts started arising in the horse's mind, "Is that right? It might be, if it is being said in such a loud voice!" The moment the horse started thinking, he started slowing down and as he slowed down he found himself surrounded by more and more donkeys all braying in their loud voice, "It is not us, it is you who is a donkey!"

'The more the horse heard this, the more he thought, "Is that right? It might be, if it is being said by so many!"

'Everyday as the horse woke up to run, it heard the same words and as he listened he went slower and slower, thinking, "Is that right? It might be, if it is being repeated every day!"

'And one day, the horse stopped and finally thought, "It is actually right, otherwise it would not have been said *so loudly*, *repeatedly* and *by so many*!"

'And since then the horse believed it and behaved like a donkey and made sure to tell every passer-by, "It is not you who is a donkey, it is me!"

She stopped and looked into my eyes and suddenly we both burst into laughter. We laughed for a long time without any inhibition. After all, it was one of those rare moments when I could laugh without feeling the pressure to look good.

It did not matter whether Ira's stories were ordinary or not, they always made an effort and in the world of Ira that was what mattered. But, sadly, not in the *Rings*. In the *Rings*, there was no place for anyone who tried and failed and that's what the guru of acting said – a second may be a second but the place in the scabbard is only for one sword.

Twenty

~

'I too am taking the test,' I spoke, trying to look confident as Geoga and Verona stared at me with surprise.

We had travelled far away from the bustle of the *Rings* on one of the roads which ran along the borders of Jewel Hill and were now sitting amidst a cluster of coral rocks.

A few months had passed since Ira had narrated her inspiring fable and with each passing day my confidence, and in turn my performance, had shown a remarkable improvement. Just today the guru had announced the names of people who were to leave his academy halfway. Thankfully, all three of us had successfully managed to avoid the misfortune.

However, a much bigger challenge was around the corner. In a few days, the guru was to conduct a test and choose the people who, according to him, would be the most serious contenders in the *Rings*. Once selected, these people were to be separated from the rest and trained exclusively. Such selection happened only twice a year – one now and one six months later.

As each student was allowed to attempt the test just once, only those who thought they were fully prepared participated now, the others waited cautiously for the second chance.

We had assembled to discuss each other's decisions.

'I am taking the test,' Verona was the first to reveal, something we all had anticipated.

I looked towards her with slanted eyes. During the last four months the three of us had become very close friends, knowing each other's strengths and weaknesses. And what I had come to know of her, no matter what the circumstances were, Verona would have taken the test at the first instance. In fact, if there was a test even before that, she would have taken that too. In a way, Verona was similar to the Baker's Wife – convinced of her eventual destiny.

'I too am going for it.' I was the second one to disclose, my face brimming with newfound confidence.

Geoga and Verona turned their heads, slightly surprised and stared at me. I did not even blink.

Had I become so confident of my acting abilities? Perhaps, no. In truth, if Verona had refused, I, too, would have done the same. Nobody knew, but she had started to occupy a very special place in my heart.

No, do not think that I did not learn from my previous failure. I did, and hence I had no intention of disclosing what I felt for her... until the right time. As of now I just wanted to spend as much time with her as possible, a desire that had flared my growing confidence.

'But I am still not ready.' Geoga took some time before finally unveiling his choice. He sounded sombre. Maybe, the prospect of getting separated from his friends, even only for a few months, had saddened him.

'You may loose,' Verona said looking at me. She seemed a bit concerned and I liked the fact that she was worried for me.

'Maybe he can win,' Geoga replied while throwing washed up pieces of coral back into the sea.

I did not reply.

It may not have been the most convincing answer but it was something that pleased me – it pleased me that my best friend believed in me. I did not probe further. What was the need? After all, in the time of arguments don't we prefer to stop when we reach a pleasing state instead of continuing to listen to disconcerting rationales?

Twenty-one

~

'Number 23 on the stage!' the guru shouted. The decisive moment had finally come.

As the last actor made a shameful exit as one more failure, I stood up and walked nervously towards the empty stage, which now appeared to me like a large sea full of man eating fish. No matter how much I assured my heart, it refused to yield to my orders of calming down. I tried hard but could not get hold of my newly found confidence which, having betrayed me, had absconded to an elusive hiding place.

The deadly stage had already spelt the fate of more than twenty aspirers and nobody except Verona had been able to leave it unwounded. I was astounded at the difficulty of the test. To me some of the performances were exemplary, but had still failed to impress the guru.

Verona was the only one who had managed to cross all the hurdles and attempted the 'Pyramid Test'. Whether she laughed as a betrayer or cried as a beloved, whether she enacted a widow or depicted a conspirator, she made the boundary between reality and acting blur many times. In fact I had a strong sense of jealousy when she enacted a love scene as if it was for real ... and as if she was actually in love with me.

With watchful steps, I reached the centre of the stage and looked towards the crowded ground. I was surprised at how everything appeared alien. As part of my training, I had performed on that stage umpteen times but now it felt as if I had never stepped on it before; the faces that I saw everyday appeared strange, as if I was seeing them for the first time. What's more, it felt that my rational master had started shouting from his room that choosing acting as a career was the biggest mistake I could ever make.

'Start!' The voice of the guru pierced my ears. I heaved a sigh and shut my eyes.

'Hey, you! Stop dreaming you swine and get the rice!' Uncle ridiculed me in his terse style. Although my body was performing, the fear of failure had transported my mind back to my village ... right into my uncle's shop.

'*Look!*' The discussing group at the Market Corner pointed towards my mother and whispered mockingly, '*She is the mother of the boy who ran away from his house ... hahaha ... the son of a failed painter who thought he could conquer the world!*'

'Stop!' Time, the deceitful shopkeeper, had barely taken out his crafty weighing scales from his bag when I heard that ominous voice.

My dreamy eyes refused to open out of the fear of encountering reality ... I wished my ears could have done the same.

I just heard the word 'rejected' out of the entire criticism and rushed down the stage. I ran like a timid fox leaving the glittering street of mirrors; towards Ira's classroom, even though the path looked blurred to my hazy eyes.

I somehow reached the shore but my feet were shocked as they went deep into the sand – that the Island's beach was made of quicksand, before today, they had never realised.

※

I had come a long way walking aimlessly on the seashore; leaving the Gateway of my dreams far behind. Tired and lonesome, I fell on my knees; I tried hard to hold the sand in my fists but in vain. The wind was helpless in wiping my tears. I wept without caring what the blatant sea would think. For hours I sat on the deserted coast staring at the returning boats and imagining myself returning to my village like a loser... walking everyday on the Kingsway to the Market Corner, passing the scornful whispers to reach the mocking master. Oh! How humiliating it felt.

I raised my eyes and gazed at the sun which was eager to set, in spite of my repeated requests it did not stay but faded away.

I lay there, helplessly seeing the sky getting darker when my ears heard familiar footsteps. Ira could be the only one who could console me in such a time of despair but that day I doubted even her capabilities.

'The sun has set. Everything is finished,' I spoke to the sea after a long silence.

'Just by the waning of the sun?' Ira also replied to the sea.

'Can't you see? The most powerful star has gone,' I answered with slight irritation.

'If so, you must hear the tale of "The impatient Sea and the pompous Sun" that is being narrated in the Crooked Tail since generations, and then decide,' replied Ira.

I was surprised. She really was strange! Here I was reduced to pieces, and she? She was only interested in telling her fabricated stories.

Ira started without paying any attention to my impassive face, 'This legend goes back... way back... to the time when the sun of this island was young and so was this sea... to the time when all parts of this island including the Crooked Tail were equal in terms of prosperity. It was an unbelievable time. You know why? Because it was a time when the sun never used to set on this Island. Yes, never – every hour, every minute, every second, the powerful sun proudly beamed over the happy Island.

'Although the sun glimmered in the sky, it knew very well that it had a quiet admirer on the earth in the form of the vast sea. The sun shone brightly above. Below, the sea told stories of its supremacy to the people. As time passed by, their friendship grew and they became best friends.

'One day, the sea saw a few young children playing with a ball – it was the first time that the sea had seen a ball and it got so fascinated that it wanted to have it straight away. As soon as the children left, leaving the ball behind, the sea grew impatient, it tried desperately to extend itself to reach the ball that rested a little farther on its shore but was unsuccessful. The sea tried and tried, but in vain!

'In the meantime, the sun was shining as usual over the Island, when it heard the sea lamenting.

'Seeing it weep, the sun spoke, "Oh Sea! You cry in spite of being friends with the most powerful in the world. What is it that you want? Nothing is beyond the reach of the almighty sun!"

'Listening to the sun, the sea wiped its tears and expressed its desire happily to its friend. The sun laughed at its friend's trivial demand and proudly swelled and started shining more brightly so that it could expand the sea. To the sun's utter surprise its powerful shine had no effect on the sea. Furious, the sun swelled more and more but could only extend the sea by a bit.

'The sun was so stunned and angry at its inability that it started causing mayhem in the flourishing Crooked Tail. Everything was destroyed in a matter of hours and then the fuming sun returned to the heavens, never to come back. For hundreds of years the ruined Crooked Tail remained under the dark clouds, but one day a tiny moon limped into the sky. The sea compared the arched moon to the mighty sun and laughed. Everyday, the sea repeatedly challenged the moon with the same request to which it listened but remained quiet. But one day when the moon grew to its full size, it smiled looking down and told the sea to expand as much as it could. With disbelief, the sea tried and to its surprise it was able to extend itself and engulf the ball. And then, God summoned the sun and commanded it to share the sky with the moon.

'Since then, everyday, as the sun leaves the sky, the sea of this Island extends itself to tell the world not to agonise and to always believe that nothing happens if one sun sets, as the other is just waiting in the heavens to emerge.'

I was confident that it was one of Ira's own stories and not a legend as she claimed and Ira knew that I knew. I also think that most of her stories were conceived on-the-spot by using elements present around her. Even now, how cleverly she thought of lunar tides while she was in front of the sea.

I stayed quiet and so did Ira, holding my hand. I did not ask but she made sure she stayed until the next sun eventually decided to stretch its arms.

Twenty-two

'The tears of defeat are not to be spent... they are to be saved for fuelling forthcoming battles.' The man sitting on the streets wanted to continue reading but stopped, as I stood, threw a few coins at him and moved ahead. I had got what I needed from him; besides, with the little time I had, every minute was precious.

Our stay at the acting academy was coming to an end. 'Pyramid Test' – the ultimate evaluation of one's acting abilities could now happen any day. It had been almost a year since the second selection took place. Geoga, who had prudently avoided the first test had successfully made his way into the exclusive training camp through the second one.

With Verona and the few others, he was now getting the best preparation. I, along with the remaining many, was going through the routine.

Although everyone in the academy was allowed to take the pyramid test, all eyes were to be only on the ones from the selected group.

But... I had different plans.

I reached the secluded end of the shore where the eager camera waited for me with its tired eyes. Yes, tired! Because since that day of my failure its eyes were not allowed to switch off even for a single day. Everyday they were compelled to stare at a determined boy, who relentlessly practised in front of them without bothering whether it was day or night. In fact, I was now fully convinced that the camera understood me better than any of my acquaintances. It was all part of a plan. Initially I was reluctant and shy to let the camera see all my emotions, but soon I realised that my reluctance was useless. Nothing could escape its powerful eyes. After every rehearsal I used to sit with the camera and be amazed at how easily it caught flaws in my acting. Soon, I realised that the only way to trick the camera was to make its eyes tired. Hence, since then I made it see me enacting emotions for so many times and with such minute precision that it not only started losing interest in those repetitive acts but also got tired of such continual alertness.

To attempt the test at the first instance was a big mistake, I had realised lately. I had underestimated the amount of effort it required to emerge as a shining true pearl. But then, if the world could be won only by confidence and ambition, every teen would have ruled it.

In spite of toiling for the past one and a half years, I knew it would not be easy to perform beside the exclusively trained aspirers of the academy. I had heard from Verona and Geoga about the rigorous training they all went through. I listened to their stories of practising together with a pinch of salt. In fact, if somebody else would have been in my place, he would surely have given up, but I had the support of Ira. And whenever clouds of doubts started to gather, I was made to remember her Horse and Donkey fable. The choice was simple, either to concede defeat and believe that I was a donkey or to keep faith in the fact that one day the world would realise that I was nothing else but a champion horse.

The decisive day finally arrived.

The large ground of the academy was full of nervous, anxious aspirers. In a few minutes from now, many of us were to abandon our dreams. Soon we were to realise that being the children of the destitute we had committed a terrible mistake by turning away from their understated but dependable destiny.

Everyone from the small selected group including Verona and Geoga was to take the test on the big stage. The remaining aspirers were to perform from the ground itself.

Standing among hundreds, I looked around. Their tense faces clearly showed that even before taking the test, they had already forfeited their claim to the *Rings*... maybe they all needed to listen to Ira's fables.

I raised my eyes and stared at the stage. No doubt, the ones performing on it had an advantageous position, so what? Weren't the elevated shopkeepers of the Market Corner in a better situation than the pushcart farmers who sat on the dusty ground? And wasn't this the reason that made the shopkeepers complacent?

If I could ever get a chance to compel the shopkeepers to look towards the ground, it was today.

'Start!' the guru shouted, as I prayed to God and shut my eyes with determination.

For a few seconds it felt as if nothing happened. But suddenly everything around me started falling quiet. And in that silence, I heard the sound of wind blowing over hot, melting earth. It was coming from far... very far. Soon, the sound grew louder and I started sweating profusely; it felt as if the temperature had leapt up by tens of degrees. I tried hard to hold my feet firmly to the ground, as the wind grew stronger and stronger.

My eyes! Never in the past had I realised what powers they had! They had flown me thousands and thousands of miles away to the middle of a forlorn desert. I rolled my eyes in amazement as there was no one around . . . no humans . . . no insects. And then everything became dark. Very dark.

Oh! Have you seen anything darker than the darkness? I did on that day!

Suddenly the darkness faded and I found myself standing very close to a huge pyramid. To my utter disbelief, the stones of the pyramid appeared alive and babbling amongst themselves.

Like one hypnotised, I walked towards the pyramid and moved my face closer to one of the walls. The stones of the pyramid were emitting heat that felt like lava. It was painful, still I wanted to hear what the stones were saying. Initially, I could not understand, but soon it became clear. The stones at the bottom half of the pyramid were unanimously warning:

You have only one life, like we had only one chance to get laid in this pyramid. Hence, make sure you rise as high as you can. Otherwise, for generations you will have to sit at the bottom like we lie under the burden of those who luxuriously and cleverly got fitted at the top.

The pain had become unbearable and hence I tired moving away from the stones but could not; my feet were glued to the ground. I tried and tried but it was in vain. I hadn't experienced death before but I was sure it was near! Unable to bear the pain, my body sagged.

My eyes opened.

Out of the hundreds fallen on the ground only three had managed to make the pyramids talk!

With curved lips I looked towards Verona and Geoga who responded with a smile submerged in amazement.

The three best friends were ready to challenge the *Rings*!

It was like God's vehicle was waiting at the check-post of the Island for the Pyramid Test to end, for, everything changed the moment the results came out.

The three of us stepped on the street of mirrors only to find that invisibility inflicted us no more. The news must have sneaked into God's vehicle and had managed to travel all around the *FameGate*, as heads kept turning and whispers intensified with each of our marching steps. This time it was for real. Each of the mirrors on the street now displayed nothing but our proud image. Oh! The old woman had already mentioned it but I realised only now – nothing can be more intoxicating than the first sip of recognition.

Finding themselves gripped in Verona's velvety palm, my fingers trembled with pleasant astonishment! Although the three of us walked together, she had shifted a fraction closer to me. Soon, my entire self was engulfed in her seductive fragrance.

Whispers turned into loud cheers as we neared the poles, but still could not bury the magical words that trickled out of Verona's eager lips into my ear.

God truly likes to give in pairs!

Twenty-three

~

The winds in the Island of True Pearls vibrated with excitement as never before!

As if we three friends were born with a destiny written by golden hands, our preparations had accomplished results just at the right time.

One of the most successful filmmakers of Jewel Hill had stirred the dreams of the aspirers at the *FameGate* with a fascinating declaration. For the past few days the mirrors were showing nothing else but his announcement, in which he was inviting everyone to the *Rings,* to be part of his most ambitious, most expensive film ever. The amazing part was that the entire cast and the crew of the film were to be selected exclusively from the *Rings*!

The filmmaker had reserved the *Rings* for one full day for his selection, which itself was to happen in the most grand style.

The enthralling news had enkindled even such desires that had been doused and buried for a long time. Old-time struggling actors, unprepared newcomers, they all were getting ready to test their kismet.

And in all this frenzy, the three newly crowned champions were getting treated in the *FameGate* as the most favourable contenders for the leading roles. Whichever path we treaded, we found strange eyes offering familiarity . . . trying their best to make us remember them.

On the other hand, the magical words from Verona had bulldozed through every cage that had imprisoned our feelings for each other. *When we win, we will not climb to the heaven sitting inside the chariot but waving to the crowd; soon, every gate of the island will have a statue of ours; when we marry, the island will see its most regal chariot ride ever.* With each passing day our intimacy reached new heights and so did our dreams.

However, there was one hitch in this perfect script and to discuss that the three of us had assembled near the coral rocks, probably for the last time.

Sitting beside the splashing waters, we looked towards the sky, which had started getting covered with a number of soaring balloons. The decisive day was still a night away, but the area near the *Rings* was already overflowing with people.

Our hesitation to speak was enhancing the stillness of the rocks. 'We are friends. And will remain so.' At last I broke the silence. We had lived long enough in the Island to know that the treacherous cobra belonged to no one. If the three of us had a chance of winning in the *Rings*, there was an equal chance of us faltering at the final frontier. What if it was to be me? Or Verona? Or Geoga?

Our meeting was to assure each other about our loyalty. That even if one of us failed, he would get lifted into the heavens on the shoulders of the other two.

Nobody spoke further. Geoga smiled, in a reassuring way . . . perhaps because he knew that out of the three of us, his position was the weakest. Verona and I were already intimate enough to help each other.

I will not lie, finding Geoga vulnerable that day, even for a moment, deep inside I felt a sense of satisfaction. Not for any other reason, but because it was for the first time that I had found him wanting.

According to me, Geoga was to be one of the strongest contenders in the *Rings* and his vulnerability showed that he thought the same about me.

I smiled back.

There was no question in my mind whether I was to be loyal to the other two – after all, one was my childhood friend and the other was the one I now trusted more than I trusted my own self.

Twenty-four

~

The sun was about to rise and I knew that from this day it would never set on me again. I sat near the sea dressed and all prepared, with my fists full of sand, my eyes sparkling with determination and my ears filled with the sound of the distant drums urging me to come soon. I knew they were desperate; the story of the three finest swords flashing in the *Rings* had travelled to every corner of the Island:

> *You know, they look like gods from heaven.*
> *Geoga?*
> *I have heard he can dance for many days without stopping.*
> *And the other one?*
> *Oh! People say his acting can make pyramids talk.*
> *But nobody compares to Geoga when it comes to physique.*
> *I have heard he can fight with hundred bulls at one go.*
> *And Verona?*
> *Oh! One day she made the departing ships return! Standing near the sea she emitted such radiance that sailors mistook her for the lighthouse flashing warning signals!*

God has been kind to provide us with the opportunity of seeing these three live; I am telling you at least one of them will become one of the most famous stars of all times.

It seemed that the *Rings* had never raised that much excitement in the past! By now, thousands of people had gathered near the foothill, all wanting to catch a glimpse of the one who would rule the world in future.

I raised my eyes and looked towards the sea. There was something in its water, something strange, as with each year on the Island, my hunger for fame had doubled.

I had resigned from Ira's job the day I succeeded at the academy. When I told her about my decision, she just smiled and like a good employer, praised me for my contribution. I am not certain how I helped Ira but in a way I enjoyed what she asked me to do. In the beginning itself, I had realised that ordinary bait would not catch and bring those young boys to school. Hence I resorted to my shopkeeper tactics. I spent every night creating larger-than-life stories, which could be told to these kids the next day. Like a skilled salesman, I waited for them as they returned from the sea or hid myself behind the heaps of fish at the fish market fearing that the servants of the merchant might see me. At the first opportunity I told them my fabricated stories...

Yes, the famous merchant was able to buy his first ship because he could draft a very clever bidding contract... and you know how that footballer found the most beautiful woman? Because he could write fancy love letters.

As a parting bonus, Ira told me her last fable. I listened to it and quickly forgot... without realising what significant role it was to play in my near future.

As I sat there deep in thought, the sea started changing colours. I stood and raised both my hands, holding the sand firmly in my hands. Soon I was to leave the earth and enter the fascinating world of true pearls but before that I knew I had a dream to fulfil – to return flamboyantly to the valley of yellow flowers exactly as the famous king did once.

Twenty-Five

~

Arched eyebrows, broad forehead, long curly hair swaying on the wide shoulders... oh... who are they who glitter more than anybody around?
As if they have mistakenly come to the ground.
Are they the ones who lived in an unknown valley once?
Look at the king-like confidence visible in their shaped eyes, the warrior-like smile resting on their full lips!
The way they wave those strong arms wrapped with beautiful bands, Jewel Hill is sure to get stormed!
Number 23... Geoga... Number 23... Geoga!!!

The *flies* buzzed, as Geoga and I marched towards the *Rings* with our hands on our waist and eyes fixed at the gates of heaven. Oh! How we pretended to ignore the ones who cheered; how we showed helplessness when they broke the fence and mobbed us!

The flurry around the *Rings* was an incredible sight... as if the entire Island had gathered to witness the unfolding of our destiny.

Covered with sparkling ribbons and floating clouds the open hood hissed as never before. The pavers of its Golden Passage bore a new shine as if the snake had gone through moulting, shedding its older skin.

True Dummy **143**

We paused near the longest-ever queue of aspirers waiting to enter the *Rings*, as our heads moved in search of Verona.

Soon, our eyes stopped at a glittering body barely enwrapped in red silk moving towards us! Never before had Verona looked so beautiful! She came closer and stood beside us, instinctively my hand rose to cover my eyes... to save them from the astonishing glow that surrounded her face.

Suddenly, the entire area was enveloped by a strange silence; all eyes rose towards the guarded gate.

People occupying the skies were the first to spot the balls of white light which blazed down the Golden Passage. They screamed, almost jumping out of their balloons, broadcasting the arrival of the filmmaker to the island, like monkeys who jump up and down shaking the branches to announce to the jungle that the tiger is arriving.

A train of chariots emerged from the sparkling scarlet gem and rolled down the open hood, as the drums thumped, the fences bowed, the streak swayed vehemently and appeared exactly like the rolling hills did the day the king inaugurated the church.

No sooner had the chariots halted and lined up at one corner of the *Rings*, the lords ordered the proceedings to start.

ೞ

I am certain that the *Rings* would not have witnessed such merciless bloodshedding before. Whether on the *right side* or the *left*, nobody could stand in front of the ruthless blade of those who descended from the heavens. The queue of aspirers was getting diminished with such speed as if the *Rings* were nothing but a bottomless pit waiting to engulf them.

As unbelievable as it may sound, many of the aspirers who had come prepared to enter the *right side* could be seen requesting the lords to let them join the group assembled on the *left*. Scared of the heartless killing, they were now happy to enter the heavens as extras as long as they could enter at all.

However, this did not apply to the group of aspirers with whom Geoga, Verona and I stood; I knew everyone around us had only one side on their mind. Our Guru had told all the strong contenders to enter the *Rings* together. It surprised us initially but we were convinced when he explained – this is the best way to hold the capricious eyes of the filmmaker for maximum duration.

We cheered and motivated each other, as the queue moved ahead rapidly but the tricky situation made the conflict apparent on our faces... we had to be together to increase our chances, yet fight amongst ourselves to emerge as the best.

Soon, we all reached the entrance and were examined by the 'assistants'.

I sighed.

The time had come.

One by one the people in front of us entered the *Rings*.

Geoga and Verona had already entered the *right side* and I was about to follow when my feet paused for a second. I rubbed my chest – there was nothing left in it but the burning flame that wanted me to be like the mighty king who named every street on which he walked or the wealthy merchant of the island who had written his name on every ship that touched its waters.

I leapt into the *Rings*.

With loud snarls we spread about like leopards inside the *Rings* and began to show the 'gods' why we deserved to enter the heavenly mount.

Can you hear the sound of the swords clashing? Feel the dust storms rising? See the blood spilling? One after the other, the deadly blade of the filmmaker moved through the dreams of the challengers, who now lay on the ground with mud covered bruises. The remaining continued, not caring whether they returned from the *Rings* dead or alive as long as they managed to show the skills they possessed.

The guru as usual was right; our pack had managed to stay in the *Rings* the longest and as his most worthy pupils we had managed to attract the maximum attention.

Verona no doubt had emerged as the undisputable queen of the *Rings*; it seemed she carried on her waist an earthen pot full of intoxicating smoke, as the crowd swayed with every move of her seductive body.

Verona... Verona... Verona... !!!

Soon, like loyal customers, they started chanting the name of the *spirit* that had allured them like no one before.

Aspirers came and went but Verona, Geoga and I stayed there mesmerising the spectators with our acting skills.

They swayed like thin branches in love with the pleasing breeze whenever Geoga showed them his dancing skills. They roared like soldiers desperate to attack the enemy whenever I went near the ropes and challenged them like an able commander.

Slowly the queue grew thinner and thinner and eventually a time came when no one on the island was left with the strength to face the lethal axe of the *Rings*... except the two childhood friends and the almost crowned queen.

In the next few minutes it seemed that Geoga and I went through several cycles of births. The instructions kept emerging from the chariots, the 'lords' directing us to keep enacting various roles. Sometimes we pounced like fighters thirsty of each other's blood, sometimes embraced each other as long-lost brothers reuniting.

This continued for some time but soon, it became ominously clear that the filmmaker had the intention of choosing either one of us.

But we were neck to neck in our display... we proved to be mirror images, almost replicas of each other, so who was to be the last sacrifice? Perhaps, it was to boil down to that one factor about which even the vendors of wisdom had no clue – the destiny.

Suddenly, the gong sounded.

The three of us stood in line close to each other... as we always did as friends before.

The black horses started flaring their nostrils and twitching their muscles in anticipation of retreat, as the 'lords' stood with their heads bowed near the chariots for the last time, listening to the names of the newly crowned true pearls.

Soon they returned followed by the four smiling servants carrying the newly decorated, bejewelled, open palanquin, as the crowd waited with bated breath.

VERONA was the first name to be announced! And as if her name had some magical power, the clouds burst and started showering red petals.

The spectators hysterically started chanting my beloved's name, as I turned my head and looked at Geoga... to reassure that I was still with him. To my surprise, he was not looking at me but at the palanquin in waiting.

True Dummy 147

GEOGA... yes, Geoga was the other name to be declared!

I was shocked, I closed my eyes and my hand intuitively moved to hold Verona's hand... but I had to withdraw immediately due to startling pain!

I opened my eyes in a flash and looked towards my bleeding hand with shock... the very same delicate palm that a few days ago embraced my fingers had suddenly turned into a sharp claw to slash the very same refuge!

My head began to spin as I saw Verona arm in arm with Geoga heading towards the palanquin. I tried holding on to my senses and ran towards them through the rain of red petals, screaming loudly with hatred.

Had Verona turned into Jula?

Had Geoga turned into my uncle?

I tried moving further but was lost in the mob. I frantically tried to look out but was stunned to see *them* again!

Jula's eyes?

Remember Jula's eyes? Thousands of Jula's eyes... breaking through the fence and swarming the *Rings* and passing me to rush towards Geoga and Verona as if I did not exist.

Holding each other's hands, Geoga and Verona entered into their chariot, as I gathered myself and rushed towards them piercing the maddening crowd, my face now dripping with agony.

The chariot turned towards the Golden Passage and started moving towards the heaven and I, along with thousands of others ran behind it. To others, the red petals may have appeared pleasant, but to me they felt like drops of blood. I even pushed aside some people so that I could prevent them from getting drenched with blood, only to be angrily slapped in return.

As the chariot reached the gates of heaven, the people behind the barricades started screaming the two names in unison. They were really unaware of the truth. Weren't they? Verona's name could only be taken along with mine... after all, she was *my* lover who had promised to remain the same in all subsequent births.

I moved in anger towards those who were screaming, to scratch their uninformed faces, when suddenly the gates of heaven opened!

To the *couple*, it must have felt like unfolding arms of God but to me the opened gate seemed like the open mouth of the large cobra threatening me with its hiss.

And right when Geoga and Verona entered the heaven, their *friend* got kicked by the cruel gatekeepers and tumbled onto the blood-splattered streak only to trip back to the earth!

Twenty-six

~

O earth! Standing here, I beg you to part...to part and take me inside....take me inside to crush my soul...crush my soul so that it can never reincarnate...eat this vain body so that it can never be repossessed. Why are you not replying? Why are you quiet? Oh, I realise! What can you do...even you are held by the unseen claws...the claws of existence. Being the mother of all, you may have to bear the curse of eternity, but release me...as, by now you must have known that I am nothing...nothing else but your insignificant son.

The *Rings* stood deserted, in darkness. The show had ended. The two new pearls had left taking everyone along...except the one who lay miserably in one dark corner of the *right side* staring at the skies and slowly losing his consciousness.

My eyes closed and the dreadful night began...bringing frightening images...all jumbled. I have turned into a dummy pearl and am getting thrown into a bonfire near the rocky beds by the old woman of the mela. I scream, I plead, as it gets unbearable...but she does not listen, just laughs hysterically. Surprisingly, she is not alone, but surrounded by people – my uncle, Geoga, Verona in her blood red gown... and Jula.

Suddenly, I see myself inside the valley... lying bruised on the white trails. Then a mad woman in tattered clothes being stoned by the important people of the Market Corner. I see her face. *Is that you, mother?* I see myself asking her in disbelief. Has she turned mad? Oh, what have I done to her! I try to get up and plead with her to come home, but she is not listening, she looks as if she does not know me. And then I see people of the Market Corner moving towards me with a yoke! *No, do not mount it on me... I am not meant to be tethered*, I request. But they do not listen; only keep talking amongst each other.

And then I imagine myself standing in the *Rings*, surprisingly winning and rushing towards the Golden Passage with my head held high, but all of a sudden Verona emerges from nowhere and sprinkles blood everywhere, throwing the last gush on my face and I fall on the ground in shame. The scene repeats and keeps repeating throughout the night.

Slowly the images get replaced by some faces hovering over.

Lords of the *Rings* arriving the next morning?

A loud voice shouts, 'Impostor! How dare he enter the *Rings* without our permission?'

'Let's throw him on the side of the extras,' someone suggested.

The loud voice was adamant, 'No! He has defied the rules of the *Rings*. Throw him near the sea and make sure he is never seen here again.'

With half-open eyes, I see them carrying me like a dead animal. I wanted to resist... to beg... *please, do not close the doors of heaven; someone is waiting there for me.*

But who was listening... who has ever listened?

&

I regained consciousness to find myself lying dejected on pebbles near the sea. With no strength left, I just looked around. I had been thrown in one of the obscure corners right at the back of Jewel Hill, which was far less beautiful than its front. There was no golden passage, just an unpaved trail winding from bottom to top on a scaly, blackish landscape. A thin queue of people could be seen crawling up, towards the strong iron gates at the top of the hill. Apparently, these people were from Crooked Tail who worked as servants of heaven... but, I was surprised to see their destitute, unhappy faces and ordinary clothes as shouldering the palanquin, they always appeared prosperous and happy.

My question was soon answered, as I looked at the Iron Gate; all the people when entering, were made to wear a good-looking dress and their faces painted to give them a joyful look. My eyes rested on the ones coming out; as they handed their dresses to the gatekeepers and removed their make-up, they looked no different from me. Strangely, the last role given to me in the *Rings* had been that of a poor farmer. With bare feet, torn clothes, messy stubble, uncombed hair and all glossiness stripped, I must have resembled my failed father. Geoga's last role in the *Rings* was that of a king.

Poverty should have been easy to enact but perhaps, it is always a king who wins in the end.

I remained there for hours trying to understand what hurt me most – losing the chance to become a true pearl or the betrayal in love?

Besides, what was the urgency... a death now and a death in few hours could not be different from each other.

Yes, death!

After all, what was the point in living with a broken heart and disloyal dreams that could never be fulfilled?

And is there a place on earth where one can live without encountering stories of true pearls?

So, death was what I had chosen!

And how an insignificant person like me dies is again immaterial. What greatness will I achieve by dying a natural death? Waste some people's time who will gather to throw me in a randomly chosen pit? Will it not be far better to jump into this ocean and become food to fish? At least they might remember me for one evening with a thankful heart.

As the sun started to set, I struggled to stand and limped slowly towards the last row of rocks.

I sat near the shore waiting for the area to become deserted. It was that time of the evening when the servants returned home and I did not want to give my life a chance.

It was an odd sight watching them jump, one after the other, into a hole. I now realised why the boulevard felt hollow with all those strange noises coming from underneath. There was no visible road from the back of Jewel Hill to the Crooked Tail or... perhaps, no one actually wanted these people to be seen in the important areas of the Island; and hence created a separate passage – a tunnel running below the boulevard only opening somewhere inside the Crooked Tail!

Soon the time came when the hole had gulped them all.

Now, there was no reason to wait.

I stood up and was about to jump when I saw the sea staring at me strangely with its newfound eyes. My feet paused, as the eyes looked familiar – satisfied, lively, meaningful. I knew from where the old sea got such young eyes. They belonged to Ira and they were reminding me of her last tale.

·'Life is like a game of chess, which you have to play even after losing the king!' she had said philosophically.

I had gone to her to resign from my job but strange as she was, she had asked me to play a game of chess.

'Before you leave, I want you to listen to my last fable – A fable of Death!' She said caressing my head with her palm. I was not interested, but it was Ira – She started without waiting for my consent:

'There was a time when this island was not an island. Till wherever the eyes could see, existed only land.' She held my hand and spoke characteristically, 'And this vast piece of land was ruled by one king. A king who was extremely fond of flowers.

'At first, this king had a small garden with a limited variety of flowers but as the years passed, the king's passion for flowers grew and his garden became larger and larger. First, to accommodate his garden he razed his palace to the ground and then this town and when even this did not satiate his desire, he turned towards the woods.

'For the king the garden was a source of joy but for others – a message of destruction; as soon as they heard that the king's garden was heading in their direction, they fled from their villages.

'The king loved his garden more than his life and trusted nobody with it and thus, watered the flowers himself. People say that a day came when his garden became as large as this sea. To water such a huge garden, the king made a big bucket and woke up every morning to do nothing but water his flowers all day long. Even though the bucket was large, it took him one full year to water his entire garden.

'With time, the king started worrying more and more about his flowers and was so caught up in safeguarding them that he forgot to enjoy their beauty. As the years passed, the king found himself caught in a vicious cycle – a day's rest and the garden shrank, if the garden would shrink, his years of hard work would be lost.

'Soon, he became terribly frustrated with his work and started finding it the biggest burden of his life. Yet, the king was not able to set himself free from the lure of flowers and continued watering them with aggravation.

'One day, the king felt that the only way he could get away from this misery was by killing himself. Thinking this, he went to a mountain, closed his eyes and requested death to come and take all his sorrows away.

'After his death, as the king opened his eyes, he was surprised with what he saw. He saw that God stood in front of him with the same bucket with which he watered his flowers.

'Seeing the king awake, God spoke, "Dear king, take your bucket and resume your work."

'To which the king answered with surprise, "But God, I am dead now and away from my garden!"

'To which God finally replied, "No dear king, that is what you assumed. Death is . . . when it is caused by me. As you have brought your unfinished destiny to the skies; from now on, as long as you stay here, you will spend your time doing nothing else, but the same work for which you took your life."

'After saying this, God converted the king's garden into a vast sea and disappeared. And since then, beyond the skies, the king wakes up everyday to fill his bucket until it is full and then he cascades it onto the earth once a year in the form of rain. And regularly, the king has to shower water, even if it is not the rainy season, just to remind the people of this earth not to return to the skies until they are asked to do so.'

I knew that like all other stories of Ira, even this one was fabricated but stupidly, a sense of fear arose in my heart.

What if the king's warning was true?

Would I always remain a failure, a dummy pearl, someone who always loses in love?

To make things worse, the sky turned gloomy, as if bringing warnings from the king.

Throughout the night I roamed about those rocks like an aimless insect, not knowing how to react to those intermittent drizzles. And just before the sun's return, I reached a decision.

I gazed at the skies and then at Jewel Hill, heaved a sigh and slipped into the dark hole.

And so, with it, slipped my dreams, my courage, my hope, my chances, my everything... but not my veiled destiny. It remained near the sea, laughing, as if asking, 'How long can you avoid what has already been written?'

Twenty-seven

~

'Is there any shop around, which sells rice and is run by an old scornful shopkeeper?'

Having crossed the entire Crooked Tail with my head down, fearing that somebody might notice me, I came to its filthiest and farthest end asking the strange question to the passers-by.

How could I explain to them why I wanted to work in such a shop? And how could such people, who had never dreamt of conquering the world, understand what it feels like when one returns after being so close to heaven?

I wanted to be the most famous and now found myself amidst faces that nobody cared to notice. Nervous faces, cowardly faces, depressed faces... faces that said at the first look that they were born to lose. Their expressions so dull, they all looked the same... like the dummy pearls of the bag.

Perhaps, that end of the Crooked Tail was not even prosperous enough to have pompous shopkeepers. Maybe its proximity to large markets kept its traders good-natured.

The only market place of that end existed just for the namesake – few haphazardly arranged, small shops with poorly dressed people behind the counters. At first sight, it was clear that these were no businessmen. Their stock was old and piling up, their displays unclean. Most of these shops had old benches and chairs in front of them, occupied for the good part of the day by idlers who distracted or rather kept the shopkeepers engaged as much as they could with their nonsensical talks.

I could not find a shop that sold rice and was also big enough to accommodate an extra person but I did find a shop-cum-eatery-cum-bar which defied every business principle and yet ran pretty well.

It sold raw fish over the counter and cooked fish to the people seated on the benches and chairs in front. The place was so smelly that it was a surprise to see people sitting comfortably, eating and drinking.

I knew I could not sell rice but sitting inside that stinking shop after smelling the scented heavens was humiliating enough ... and, why forget that serving the servants of heaven was an added bonus for me?

~

He gave me an astonished look, dropping all his pretensions. He must have been surprised but surely not more than me. The Well-Dressed Man was easy to spot among the other pitiful idlers, who had started gathering on those benches from early in the morning. It was my first day in the all-in-one shop and it did not take me long to realise that the principal source of its revenue was the cheap rice wine it served. I never drank, hence, could only assume what pleasure drinking brought to these idlers. Maybe an intoxicating, falsified sense that they had escaped the clutches of their existence ... maybe a never-dying state of subtle unconsciousness, which helped them survive as insignificant pearls ... maybe something that made them think and live like wanderers without the associated troubles of getting uprooted time and again.

And he sat in the middle, reading the newspaper with all his original boastfulness, narrating stories of Jewel Hill to those drunken ears in his artificially modulated voice...

Veeerrrronaaaa (a long drag), *the new shining star* (dramatic pause) *made sure to stop her victory chariot near the coral rocks to cover a wet and cold beggar with her warm furry jacket* (pretentious nod), *an act of charity witnessed by thousands* (shrugs and rolls eyes).

Our eyes met, his arrogance vanished. But only for a moment. He might have feared that the secret that he was a failed actor who earned his living by tantalising aspirer's dreams, that he was someone who cleverly hid his past and his current place of living from the newcomers of the *FameGate* would no more remain a secret. And that he was about to be dislodged from the position he had achieved after years of juggling. But those clouds of fear cleared as soon as they gathered.

He was an experienced man. A sharp glance convinced him that I was no more in the race to the *Rings*. In fact I was now nothing more than a harmless fly... and by the law of nature, flies cannot eat flies, even if they want to.

Our eyes entered into an implicit agreement that I would not tell the world that he was nothing but just a 'Well Dressed Man' and he would not tell that I was an outcast rejected by the lords of the *Rings*.

I know I could have felt dejected or betrayed for being duped by a nobody but then the Well-Dressed Man was not anybody; in fact he was far better than me. Like the inventors of alcohol, he was credited for producing an entire breed who hid themselves behind good looking clothes and derive the same pleasures out of it as these idlers do out of drinking. And besides, he at least had a name while I had remained as anonymous as my unknown valley.

※

I am sure the worst thing in life is to cook one's own food and eat it all alone.

The wheel of my aimless life had started to roll. I will not hide from you where I stayed in Crooked Tail. In fact if I ever get a chance, I would take you to my dingy room situated far away from the three gates. My room was situated just behind the all-in-one shop over an open drain with dirty water.

I think my fear of the tether was exaggerated. Honestly, once you get into a routine, it does not feel that bad. I never worked in an office but I presumed my new work would be similar. Is it not the case that in offices people who do not have any special skills end up doing everything? My job too was like that in the all-in-one shop – washing dishes, chopping fish, cleaning benches, serving idlers and in-between offloading heavy drums of fresh catch and wine. Seriously, it was not that bad, however, I felt the worst when I returned to my room and sat all alone looking endlessly at the platter. At first, I ended up throwing all the food out of the window into the drain without realising that this acted as an invitation to street dogs that started queuing up regularly in front of my room. In a way it was good, as I now had company and a reason to return.

I think, time has fragrance hidden up its sleeves, otherwise how could it happen that as time passes, things start to stink less?

I did not realise but slowly, illusionary dreams started cropping up – me beating Geoga in the *Rings* and riding the chariot with Verona while waving off the *flies*, me returning to my village as a true pearl, Verona and Geoga arriving in Crooked Tail looking for me and apologising for their hideous act....

These daydreams gave me exactly what alcohol gave to drunkards or the shiny dresses to the well dressed ... a shell under which we all could live in our make-believe world. But make no mistake, this shell was not foolproof! No doubt it was our final layer of defence, but it was a funny sort of a defence – a shield from outside but with thorns from inside ... something that killed us yet did not kill completely ... something that lent us life yet did not let us live. I started viewing the idlers with sympathetic eyes; after all they were like me, all hiding behind this awkward shell.

And once again I began my life as a nobody, who whenever he felt anxious, whenever he saw his life as a burden, just spread out his 'present', sprinkled dreams on it, rolled it and dragged on it like a smoker ... and kept dragging on it until it became heart-rending. I went on living but somewhere in my heart I knew that the bigger punishment was yet to come and it did when my very own protective shell turned into an assassin and pierced my heart brutally. But smoking too kills, doesn't it?

Twenty-Eight

'What do you do?' At last she gathered courage and asked.
If a person has to tell what he does, then probably he does not do anything worth telling, my mind barked.

I had just started visiting that lonely part of the beach. Ironically, the owner of the all-in-one shop turned out to be a nice man. Soon, he realised that I was willing to be exploited and instead of ignoring the daily extension of my shift he compelled me to leave as soon it was time. It was actually he who had pestered me to visit this part of the ocean. At first, I was reluctant but then, water and I shared a strange relationship. Soon, I started spending my evenings watching those smiling inhabitants of Crooked Tail, playing with their children on the seashore and wondering what sins had I committed to deserve such a cruel destiny that snatched my innocence but gave nothing in return.

I noticed her a couple of days ago, strolling near the beach. She was not the kind of girl who would make heads turn – long hair, loose top, hesitant expressions, unobtrusive gestures. A look was enough to convince me that she was not even aware that a place like the *FameGate* existed in this world. She was like thousands of ordinary looking girls you see everyday on the streets... if you care to look at them, anyway.

Something told me that she wanted to talk – her wishful glances, her crossing deliberately in front of me, her mandatory smiles, all told the same story; but perhaps, my stern looks and her nervousness kept her at bay.

I was surprised when she walked towards me and spoke shyly, 'Hello, my name is Cyntha.'

I did not reply. I wonder now how she would have felt then.

My snub put her in an awkward situation. She was not the bold type. I do not know how she gathered the strength to sit down next to me and speak, 'I am new to this place. I work as a nurse. What do you do?'

It was surprising that her presence did not irritate me; perhaps she had nothing that made me feel inferior.

She had asked – what do I do. Well, what did I do? She was a total stranger but I still wanted to tell her many things... maybe her being a stranger was the reason why I wanted to. I wanted to tell her that I was one of the most sinful persons she could ever have met. I was the one who had betrayed the aspirations of his hardworking mother. I was the one who, like a fool, had squandered a lifetime scholarship for an impossible chase. I was the one who had escaped from my valley like a coward and had never cared to see whether my parents were dead or alive. I was the one who broke Saviour's heart and converted it into a mere stream. I was the one who made big promises to the red roofs and now lay shamefully in a pothole. Yes, I am the one who did so many things, Cyntha.

I remained silent.

˞

I kept meeting Cyntha over the next few days. There was nothing exciting about her but I had nothing else to do. She worked for a charitable trust which put up medical camps in deprived parts of the world. Cyntha did not remember for how long she had been travelling like this. She said she had picked it up from her parents who, like her, had travelled to the remotest places on earth in their 'hospital boat'. Yes, they had a boat on which they ran a mobile treatment-centre carrying medicines and volunteers to dangerous areas, where no ordinary doctor was willing to go. She was very little when her parents died; they had drowned while trying to cross a flooding river in a boat. Miraculously, Cyntha was saved by a ship carrying volunteers of the same charitable trust she later started working for. She was raised on the ship and stayed on.

Cyntha said that she could see her parents' shadow in the oceans.

How do I remember all this even though I had not paid attention to what she had said? I think Cyntha's nomadic life did not let her find ears that would listen to her apprehensions, her questions, her thoughts and as my ears did not show any resistance, she shared whatever she could.

Do not think I did it out of kindness. I was what I was – a spirit frozen in time. It was she who treated me as a friend, in the same way as I once treated a quiet stream, an exuberant Saviour. In fact, my surrendered ears eventually added more work to my list of tasks in the all-in-one – idlers had now started narrating their life's sordid tales to me:

It has been ten years since sister has been taking care of her handicapped husband. I ask where God is.

My grandmother is over ninety years old and suffers from memory loss, my mother takes care of her but my grandmother cannot even remember the face of one who cares for her. I ask where God is.

I listened silently. What answers could I give? These poor people were too naïve... they did not even know that all eyes are supposed to be on the glittering pearls of the bag.

And people of the Crooked Tail?

Ironically, they lived in a land that was too crooked to be spotted from the 'heavens'.

Twenty-Nine

On that ill-fated day my master's son had run away again. He was a young boy who dreamt of becoming a famous dancer and hated sitting in his father's all-in-one shop. So whenever he could, he sneaked to the golden streak. That his father would start beating him as soon as he came home was not what was bothering me. It was a routine sight – him returning all bruised after his unsuccessful attempt to stand in the *Rings* and his father lecturing him on the idiocy of his dream. In a way, my master was right; his son was absolutely ignorant of the complexity of the game. He was not even in the race, but, would he understand? Would he give up? I cared the least. Yet that day I waited for him with desperate eyes. In fact, that day I waited for every gust of wind that came from the direction of the open hood.

I stared impatiently at the cooks who were preparing the furnace for the evening and in turn were disturbing my daydreaming. What troubles they take, cleaning bricks, arranging wood, pouring oil, facing smoke and incessantly pumping air to keep the flames alive and repeating this twice everyday. I wish they knew that there would be no need to go though this pain if... if they could find one, just one heart of a lover and throw it into the furnace.

I know it will sound foolish but the Well-Dressed Man's warning– *'new lovers are like mating snakes, do not go close to them,'* had failed to scare me. Something was trying to convince me that I could win my love back and convince my friend to repent. That day the Well-Dressed Man had read what would be his last news for me.

Geoooga and Verrrrooonnnaa, the new glittering stars have announced their wedding, which is to be one of the most expensive ones in the history of the Island. The Golden Passage will again turn red for a chariot ride, which, for the first time, will go through the other side of the tunnel.

I snatched the newspaper from him and saw Verona holding hands with Geoga. Oh! How beautiful she looked in her red gown! The Well-Dressed Man gave probably his only free advice. I knew he was jealous. Fool, he did not know why my friends were bringing their chariot into the Crooked Tail.

The master's son had returned and was washing his face when I went and stood beside him. As if he knew what I wanted, he whispered with sparkling eyes and a suppressed laugh through his bleeding lips, 'Want to experience heaven?', he asked and replied in the same vein, 'It was impossible but I have managed to convince a guard. He will allow us to stand close... very close to where the chariot is planning to stop for a few minutes. Can you imagine... that we will be within a few feet of the goddess!'

Our eyes thanked each other. I was happy, as I had got the opportunity to communicate my love to Verona and he had finally found someone who applauded his worth.

We sat at the shore, me with the newspaper tightly gripped in my fist and she gazing at the sunset. I had told her about Verona and my next day's endeavour. Cyntha's words expressed their gladness, but her face was too untrained to hide its melancholy. I was surprised at this conflict. Had she secretly started harbouring something in her heart . . . something beyond friendship, something closer to love? Why should she? I never promised her the moon, sun, stars . . . I never thought about her in my loneliness . . . I never showed her fairy tale dreams? I . . .

I brushed off her feelings with indifference . . . in turn forgetting something which I myself had learnt very early in life – you do not need two people to call it love.

❧

My life had reached a decisive turn . . . decisive and fatal.

The chariot emerged from the dark tunnel with a deafening roar. We stood almost at the end of the boulevard as part of a large group slightly detached from the rest. Who would believe that one day I will have to stand behind the very same barricades I hated the most and be part of the very same fly-swatting game I had always made fun of?

That it was to come through this way, I had not imagined – our group was strategically chosen for the charity act. For the public it was to look like a spontaneous act of *'spotting the poor, stopping the chariot and giving away alms '*, but in reality it was all to be staged. We were like extras in a movie, with a pre-written script, lesser costumes, always to be in the background, coming in the frame only when the stars needed company.

As the chariot turns back, Verona will give touching expressions (yes, she has been briefed) . . . will request the driver to stop near this group, whisper in Geoga's ears, who will nod with empathy and clap for an aide. The aide will rush in (with concerned expressions) with these twenty odd blankets and pass them on to the couple. The distribution will start. You can choose between 'Thank you for the kindness' or 'May God bless your marriage'. Do not worry about the background claps; we will take care of them . . . total scene time – two minutes. Action!

We all had names in this scene; after all it was an important role. I was to be the last one to receive the blanket and hence was called 'number 23'. Yes, number 23. I had been adorned with this title earlier and what an occasion my destiny had chosen to remind me of that!

Verona's eyes overflowed with empathy; her face truly reflected the painful emotions her heart was going through. People cried as tears rolled down her pink cheeks. She rested her head on Geoga's strong shoulders who himself appeared in a distressed state. She clearly was moved seeing their pitiable condition. That is what people thought but I knew there was more to it – she was repenting losing me. And Geoga's vacant face told the same story too. For a moment, I completely forgot about the humiliation I had felt on that day and moved forward.

Never think that a cobra can only harm if its fangs pierce the skin. Those careless animals who deliberately tease it from a distance thinking that they are safe can face the unimaginable; the snake sways pretending . . . sometimes as a prey . . . sometimes as a droll, confusing the one who teases with its expressionless face and seducing it to come closer and then they see its mouth open . . . they come closer and suddenly two streams of venom emerge and penetrate their eyes gifting them with a lifetime blindness.

Verona did not recognise me until I held her wrist and tried jumping the fence. Her eyes widened and her cheeks suddenly turned blue! This was not in the script and maybe that's why her reaction was natural. I saw her mouth open and then the gush of venom.

Oh! My eyes! I do not know what went into them in that one moment, as they widened in disbelief. The last thing they saw was the master's son, his innocent face had turned pale and his eyes frozen as if they had encountered death.

Thirty

In this world,
Your blood is blue
But pale is mine.
In this world,
You are an inestimable 'pearl',
But I'm a worthless swine.
In this world,
Sleep of yours is justified,
But even my dreaming a crime
In this world,
You are a wish come 'true',
But I'm a mistake divine
Alas, in this world.

Now it was too late. The venom had left its influence. It had been two days and the master's son hadn't returned. And it did not look like he would. I too was buried somewhere in my room with the red scratches that could be seen running all over my face. At first, I tried washing off the venom... twice, thrice, many times but it was in vain. It felt as if the venom had pricked my face and entered into the veins and even my nails failed to pluck it out.

I do not know for how many hours I sat next to the window staring in oblivion, sometimes laughing, sometimes crying like a child. The poison had deteriorated my vision but in reality its fatality was deeper, it had entered my heart and had squeezed out every drop of faith.

It had started drizzling in Crooked Tail. It did not look that bad but something suggested that it was here to stay. It was a dark night, perhaps as dark as the one in which I had escaped the valley. And in that dark night, I slowly slithered towards the ocean where many cargo ships were ready to leave the drenched island on their long journey. I did not care to enquire about the direction they were heading in, nor their final destination. I knew boarding any of those was like inviting death ... but perhaps, that is what a sinful, habitual escapist like me deserved.

∾

And so he left ... left for an unknown world with his foggy eyes, with his numb thoughts, with his dying questions and with one last wish, a wish that he never survives this death-defying journey. He might have thought that his punishment was over, that he had escaped the clutches of existence but then he did not know that life was not yet ready to give up on him, as many colours of his veiled destiny were still left to be seen.

PART 3

PART 3

Thirty-one

～

Perhaps, that ship too was dejected with its existence otherwise why would it deliberately choose to sail in such terrible weather? In fact, I was now sure that while deceiving its sailors, it was cunningly taking them onto more and more treacherous courses.

For months the heartbroken ship floated, from rainy to rainier parts as if searching for a more suitable place to commit suicide.

Initially, the sailors did not know about the additional luggage they were carrying, but they soon found out. They were already frustrated with the weather and hence vent their anger on this unwanted piece... sometimes through their mouth and sometimes with their heavy boots.

As the sailors came and kicked, I lay unperturbed, just remembering the heavy boots of the guards I once saw as a young boy at the inauguration of the church. It was easy to play the role of a dead baggage; after all I was not that bad an actor.

The sailors were good people; they eventually pitied me, and started throwing their leftovers in my direction. I did not eat, I waited for the food to become stale, as the more stale it grew, the better it tasted.

Finally, one day, my feeble eyes saw a yellow glow at a distance presumably coming from a lighthouse; however, the weather was too stormy for the ship to enter the quay.

For days, the ship stood facing the lighthouse and when one day I saw sailors sailing away in a small boat I got convinced that the ship had finally chosen its place for the ultimate sin.

I remained there with the ship in the rain, quietly staring at the lighthouse. I do not remember when I slept, when I woke up – it all appeared the same. The only thing I remember are the horrific dreams I had during that time, like the one with the old woman sitting in front of the ashes, beating her head and singing a dirge ... did she know I was about to die? I was somewhat relaxed as it was the ship, not me that was doing the killing.

One day the sailors returned, they wanted to throw out some goods to make the ship lighter and save the rest. Their eyes caught me but instead of throwing me into the waters, they brought me to the shore and left me near the lighthouse. I lay there for days, staring at the ship which was trying hard to drown, from the corner of my eyes.

Eventually the ship was successful in its endeavour.

I knew it would ... after all it was not as ill-fated as the sinful me.

~

The skies cleared and I stood up; but for where, for whom?

I did not know how but yet I walked ... and kept walking. I crossed flowers, crossed lands, crossed rivers, crossed people, one location to another, in search of more poverty, more trouble, more humiliation; I made sure to do the dirtiest of jobs – cleaning sewers, burying decaying animal corpses, transporting putrid cadavers.

I passed hundreds of sunsets, hundreds of villages, but never built a house. I stayed under the trees, under the rain, in the heat, in the cold... the worse the conditions, the better I felt.

Slowly, my impeccable physique began to melt. The strong feet that I had developed over the years of toil began to shiver; the wide shoulders, the broad chest, the strong arms, it all disappeared, but what refused to get wrecked was the pain – the venom had dried and was now frozen in my veins and hence, perhaps, was keeping the soreness alive.

I do not know how, but one day I began to cry. I cried for days, for months and then the tears dried. They were gone but took my sensations along – as I felt nothing, nothing hurt after that, no pain, no cold, no heat, no rain, nothing, even my memories dried with those tears. Those years in the yellow valley, in the Island of True Pearls, that day in the *Rings*, that moment behind the barricade, it all went back behind a very, very dense smoky curtain.

I think I had finally learnt to adjust to my peculiar destiny... or was it the other way round?

୬

Everything remained the same until one morning when I was woken up by a strange but comforting dream. I saw my mother, she was feeding me with her own hands; surprisingly, instead of sitting in front of her, my head rested in her lap and then suddenly she turned into Saviour with me floating on it, with my head up and eyes looking at the skies.

Having walked for years, my purposeless journey had let me see most of God's canvas – its fortunate parts which had been painted in the best of his moods, the ones in which he had drawn as beautifully as he could, filled them with as varied colours as possible; where he spent hours detailing those mountain chains, stroking those colourful flowers, sketching those curvaceous rivers; and its less fortunate parts – the ones where it felt as if he was in a sombre mood, where he had just sketched a few lines and covered them with blue or green, creating vast oceans.

Whatever it was, he gave something or the other to every part, but this part where I had reached now appeared to be the victim of his utmost anger.

It appeared as if rather than picking up his brush, God had just glared at the empty canvas and turned it pale and grainy; what emerged was an immeasurable land of nothingness – miles and miles of forlorn desert, boiling with heat.

It was night when I touched the tip of this unfamiliar part of the earth.

Everything was draped in darkness, nothing was visible; yet the void, the emptiness could be sensed.

I saw the other travellers, the people of the desert, who were quietly moving towards what looked like a river. It had been days of continuous travel and my body wanted to rest. Despite this, my feet voluntarily turned in their direction.

I had only been part of their convoy for a few days, yet a strange force drew me towards them, maybe, because I found them similar to me – plain robes, long hair, covered heads, covered mouths as if they too did not want the world to notice their presence.

They talked little, ate little and their meaningful eyes reflected generations of struggle. Like me, they too did not have a permanent roof and they did not seem to crave for one either; few twigs of wood and a temporary fireplace was all that these people had in the name of a house.

However, there was something that distinguished me from them, something that I had lost long ago. Peace. A sense of harmony with oneself, a sense of satisfaction, which said that their way of life was nobody's but their own choice, that to be with the punishing desert was an intentional decision taken centuries ago. And this was reflected whenever I saw them singing, which they did almost every night.

Quietly, they all settled in a boat and I too occupied a corner and waited for them to start. As the wooden boat moved in search of deeper waters their voices did too. They sang slowly with a minimum of strings, staring into nothingness as if addressing the desert. I did not know what they meant, their language was unfamiliar yet I liked it.

I did not want to know what the words stood for as I feared that their meaning might be different from my own thoughts. They sang and I translated – God, if it is possible to give, give me more pain, as there are still some cracks left, very thin ones that have escaped your eyes. Please, do fill them too to make sure that my heart does not fail to turn into a complete stone.

The boat slowly sailed through the darkness and I did not realise when sleep made me its prey. My eyes opened with the strange dream, it had been years that I had seen an unsuppressed slice from my past.

I rose, gripped with a strange sense that suggested that I had been to this place before, that what was happening to me had already happened. My eyes moved. The boat was passing through a narrow creek covered with dense bushes on both sides.

The existence of a swollen river with greenery on its sides in the middle of a desert made me wonder.

'Oh, traveller...,' finding me wanting, the oarsman addressed, '...we people of the desert believe that God flows in the form of this river, as in its absence there would have been no life in the sand.'

His words brought a long-lost childhood friend in front of my eyes. Tears trickled, as I leaned and touched the serene water. I remained like that, looking at the river for a long time; my gaze was only broken when the boat started to move towards the shore.

My eyes gazed at the travellers standing near the bank waiting to board and then rested at the vast nothingness beyond – at the unobstructed skies, at the unhindered wind.

It felt as if life wanted to exist only glued to the riverbeds.

And then, my eyes were fixed on the faint outline of what seemed like a huge mountain standing far, far away.

At first I felt my eyes were being deceived, as the mountain appeared to be covered with snow, but soon the doubts were cleared.

'That is the White Mountain, made up of white sand situated in the white desert,' the oarsman said while thrusting the oar forward, 'Life in this tough desert does not get tougher than around the White Mountain.'

As the boat touched the shore, I gathered myself to alight.

The oarsman was surprised at my sudden abandoning of the journey. I smiled faintly; he would never know that it was he who gave his passenger the reason to depart.

Thirty-Two

~

It was not that God neglected the empty part of the canvas completely. It is famous in these deserts that he once rose from the river and walked through the nothingness creating specks of life wherever his large feet fell.

One only has to look at these oases to believe in this folklore; scattered arbitrarily all over the desert, appearing as if a woodcutter had sliced them out of a fertile land and pasted them onto the barren sand, these pockets of life did not look any less than a miracle.

I sat under the stars listening to the people of the desert as my caravan halted at the first oasis. True, these were not the ones I had followed to the boat but for me they were the same – their clothes, their eyes, their songs, their conduct, everything about them. Just their faces had changed.

The more time I spent with these people of the desert, the more akin I felt to them. It had been two days since our caravan had left the life-giving river to enter the merciless desert and to see these people travel quietly, patiently on an invisible, uneven path, under blistering heat, amidst winds shrieking 'death', to find these people embrace deceptive dunes, befriend threatening storms felt comforting, comforting that I had not been the only one.

One by one the oases passed, bit by bit our caravan began to shrink, little by little the surroundings became more testing; yet the people of the desert kept moving.

And one day it seemed as if everything had changed.

I woke up in the morning and opened my eyes in disbelief... it seemed that in one night our camels had discovered that they could fly and covered thousands of miles in space to take us to a different planet!

I could breathe but it felt like there was no air. I hadn't experienced death but to me this seemed to be a place to be encountered after life – a limitless sea of white sand with hundreds of mysterious-looking white rocks scattered around. And on the enormous, vacant horizon stood a huge white mountain staring back at me... as if with a smile, reminding me that I had once made the mistake of calling the mighty mountains stationary.

Small white rocks lay on the sand like mere stones, but the huge ones weirdly stood tall on narrowing plinths, defying gravity. As our caravan slowly moved in front of these huge rocks I felt as if I was not passing under the shadow of stones but of people. The uneven, oval-shaped white rocks looked like heads of humans cut off and placed on thin flute-like trunks nailed into the sand. If looked at closely, each of these white rocks seemed to have an outline of human emotion... as if a human spirit was captured and caged inside each one of them.

Soon the caravan started changing direction, a sign that an oasis was near. I looked ahead and prepared myself for the break – the White Mountain was still a long way away.

Slowly our small caravan entered one more step of God. It was only later when I saw the caravan dismantling, that I realised that it was in fact the last step of God, as no oasis existed between this one and the White Mountain.

I turned my head and stared at the skies, with no oasis in its vicinity, the White Mountain stood isolated in the midst of lifelessness and, as I later came to know, was unattainable even by the extreme standards of the desert.

It felt as if life had moved a full circle – trying to end where it began.

It felt as if I hadn't left my village at all. The Last Step of God – an unknown, unreachable, unseen place existing solely because the water wanted it to; a story written on papers which nobody cared to read. Dusty streets built by themselves, an insignificant, small market place, houses of mud... people of mud, all looking at me and screaming – what was the need?

And yes, they were right. The tree was found but where was its shadow? Where were the ones who brought me into this world, the ones who gave me that subtle sense of offhandedness? The ones who lived with me at some point of time? The ones who loved... even the ones who hated?

But then, does a woodcutter ever deserve a shadow?

Everybody had left and probably gone home, probably into somebody's waiting arms or even to crossed ones, but here I was, sitting alone on the deserted traveller's platform, the last stop in the desert where nobody assembled to go further but only to return. There I was, clinging onto the caravan and being unsuccessful... watching the bathing camels and being unsuccessful... sighing and being unsuccessful... eating my food and being unsuccessful... thinking about existence and being unsuccessful.

Did one moment pass or years?

Did I do enough or too much?

Was this death or is this what life is?

And instead of entering the oasis I stayed where I was, slowly swallowing my food, still treating myself as a traveller when a hand touched my shoulder. My mouth froze; there was something in those quivering fingers... something that suggested they were familiar.

I turned my head.

Thirty-three

~

It was Cyntha; her eyes on my face, looking for the handsome, young boy they had once known. I tried my best to enact anonymity, but perhaps even my acting was now too rusted to be of any use.

Nothing had changed in Cyntha or Cyntha's life. She was still a nurse working for the same charitable trust. A few years ago they had touched the desert never expecting that their stay in it would be so long. From oasis to oasis, they travelled with each visit stretching their imagination of poverty, and in turn their stay. They hadn't been in the Last Step for long, yet were to leave it soon. Their stock of medicines had been exhausted leaving them with no other option.

I do not know why, but at Cyntha's insistence I reluctantly agreed to extend my break. Was it because I needed more rest? Or was it the guilt of once having broken her heart? I would never be able to judge.

Cyntha and her team had camped just across the traveller's platform in front of a large barren ground, but that was only half of the reason why I was spotted. As I rose and walked into the Last Step with Cyntha, I was reminded of what my grandmother once said – someone who can sense air can sense life.

Never in the past had the air registered its presence as strongly as it did then. I raised my head and looked around, the same mud- brick houses, the same dusty streets, the same people of the desert as in all the previous oases, yet the air of the Last Step felt strange. As if there was something in it . . . something apprehensive, something that was young, something that was challenging.

It was a large animal-barn like place with a 'plus' sign hanging at the entrance. The day hadn't started, yet a small crowd of women could be seen waiting with their children in the long corridor outside.

Apart from having an open central area which looked like a temporary dispensary, the barn had a few small rooms in which Cyntha and her team were staying.

The window of Cyntha's room overlooked the traveller's platform, a place where her eyes had been focused for the past few days and why only hers? The entire oasis was desperately waiting for that one person's arrival . . . probably the reason why I was spotted, accidentally. But who he was and why everyone was waiting for him so anxiously was something in which I had no interest.

Cyntha left with the promise to return soon. I remained in her room staring at the now empty traveller's platform and wondering how she would have reacted seeing me sitting there all alone, with defeated expressions in my eyes.

Slowly, with the climbing of the sun, the barren ground started filling up. It was easy to make out that the ground was being used as a makeshift place for an open market; however, as I later came to know, only a weekly market. The oasis was too poor to afford anything more frequent.

People came and went and I remained at the window without paying much attention to anything, even so, one thing could not escape my attention – the large proportion of young children in the population.

Cyntha returned with plates of food in her hands. The table was just beside the window and I thought Cyntha would have liked looking at the marketplace while eating. But I was wrong, she did not raise her eyes even once, in fact it seemed she was deliberately avoiding looking out by keeping her head down.

Soon, it became clear that neither of us was actually interested in eating. I surprised myself by getting up and placing my hand on her shoulder.

I knew her eyes were wet.

We remained like that for a long time before Cyntha requested me to accompany her to the weekly market. It was then that she told me the reason for the large number of children in the oasis... which to me appeared as weird and as similar a reason as I had heard when I was a sixteen year old boy.

Years ago, on a bright morning, people of the Last Step woke up to a huge surprise, they saw that a young man dressed like a king was sitting on a white horse and was accompanied by a large number of subordinates on this very ground. They jumped with joy when they were told that he was none other than the young king of the desert, who had travelled all the way from the river to their oasis to shower it with a bequest.

The king requested everyone to follow him to the end of the oasis where he alighted from his horse and touched the ground. He then took its sand in his hands and announced what was to be his gift to the desert – the construction of a large school. A school with a vision to educate every child of the desert, a school that could accommodate thousands, a school that would not only provide free schooling, but also free food and free accommodation, a school that was to reduce the ethnic clashes amongst the different clans of the oases by bringing their children together and a school which was to be built on the very soil that was in his hand.

As soon as the king finished, people erupted with happiness and immediately planned a celebration in his honour to be held the day after. The king readily agreed to their request of spending the night in the oasis. Nobody knows what happened during that night, as the next morning, to everyone's surprise, the king had disappeared along with his horse, his subordinates went in all directions but could not find the king. However, they did manage to find his will, in which his successor was instructed to keep the promise.

The school was constructed as per the king's wishes and attracted a large number of children from the surrounding oases, but as is the fate of unrealistic dreams, it soon became clear that due to lack of able teachers the school's purpose was to be defeated. However, the school continued to attract hungry children who had no other chance of survival, such children whose poor parents were forced to abandon them in the Last Step because they themselves had no roof over their heads and wandered from oasis to oasis in search of food.

Everything had been going fine, but suddenly a month ago the Last Step received its worst news – a letter from the present king, who had made the decision to stop supporting the school.

It was a bad sign and the old people of the desert knew that the end of the school would not only mean the rise of the long buried conflicts among oases, but would also result in the death of many children. Hence, one day they all got together and convinced the headmaster of the school to visit the king with their request to continue supporting the school.

And thus, all eyes in the Last Step were now fixed on the traveller's platform in anticipation of that crucial news.

We kept walking quietly through the temporary lanes of the dusty marketplace. Now everything was clear – that difficult wind, those anxious old eyes, those staring young faces.

I sighed and turned towards the traveller's platform.

I could not see her but I knew she was there – my ill-fated destiny, jumping up and down with the help of my ominous feet causing clouds of luckless dust to fly and gather over the last oasis.

'What is your name?'

'How does it matter what this insignificant boy of an unknown world is called? Besides, now I do not even have to write this ordinary name on my books anymore!' Cyntha had paused near the mat of a trader and asked, to which the trader replied without raising his head.

My eyes that were fixed on the traveller's platform suddenly changed direction. It was a young, confident voice that seemed to have emerged from my past ... from that period when somebody had made me realise the difference between the two kinds of pearls.

He was an odd looking trader. A boy of about fifteen in a blue robe and a loose blue turban, sitting on the ground amidst the other much-older looking traders. However, more intriguing were the items he had up for sale.

No, these weren't the usual dates, watermelons, milk or goats, these were ... well, to see them you would have to bend your knees and lower your eyes and need to buy at least one of his items, as the boy did not seem to be the kind of vendor who would allow his customers to freely fiddle with his goods or bargain endlessly without wanting to buy. As Cyntha continued, trying to strike a conversation, I looked at his temporary holding – twelve books, ten notebooks, three pens, one pencil, one box, one bag and one uniform, all meticulously arranged.

'It is not right to sell books. What's more, the Headmaster might come with the good news,' Cyntha tried to convince the boy.

'My camel does not eat books . . . ' the boy said while touching his chest and pointing to his small camel that stood behind him, ' . . . and I do not eat free food. I came to the Last Step to learn, not to wait and die. I am selling my books so that my camel can be fed and I can be taken back to my small oasis. I know that the Headmaster will come empty-handed and then everyone will come to this market to sell their books but they do not know this simple rule of business – when everyone sells, nobody buys. Now, move along and let me concentrate on my business.'

The boy's curt and prudent businessman-like answer had made Cyntha speechless; after failing in her bargain, she had no option but to get up.

'We will buy your goods, but we have two conditions.' My intrusion had not only surprised the boy and Cyntha, but also me.

Why did I intervene?

Was it the long lost boy of the Market Corner who had spotted a bargain?

Or was it the part-time employee of Ira, who could not see a customer slip away?

I regretted as soon as I finished but the statement had been made.

'Yes, two conditions,' I spoke while acting like a confident, careless customer surprised at the ease with which I portrayed the character . . . as if my missing acting skills had suddenly returned.

'One, we will buy everything you are selling. And two, we will leave our goods in your custody until we find a suitable customer for it. Say yes...' I paused and tried to look as sure as I could, '...otherwise you know what will happen once the Headmaster arrives.' I said and started bundling his shop as if I knew he would agree.

I still do not know why I enacted that part and where I got the strength from. I wish I knew that my performance was about to put me in greater trouble.

The boy thought for a while before nodding and saying, 'All right, but I will leave this place the day our school shuts down.'

I nodded in return with a pretentious smile and glanced at Cyntha, who had already started counting money.

We hadn't walked far when we heard the boy shouting to our backs –

'Friends, people call me Sultan.'

ॐ

Even the king knew that I had arrived in the deserts with my cursed destiny and thus, dutifully returned the Headmaster empty-handed. The school was to shut down as soon as the current instalment exhausted.

Cyntha and I stood at the window overlooking the barren ground which was now bustling with many Sultans.

I raised my eyes and looked at the White Mountain; perhaps, the time had come to resume my journey and to discharge the oasis from the burden of my ominous feet.

'You must do something!' the words struck my ears suddenly.

I could feel Cyntha's strong grip around my arm while she burst forth like a child. Yes, like a child. Because it is only a child who expresses his or her craving without getting entangled into the net of reality, whose young eyes always sparkle with hope, irrespective of his or her limitations. And I could tell this with certainty . . . after all I myself had been childlike for many years.

'You can do it!' she was convinced.

Suddenly, I felt uncomfortable, as if my mind sensed that it was in danger of facing the forgotten past. My body responded like a prey about to be attacked – tensed posture, jittery toes, sinking heart.

And then the words struck, 'I saw you convincing Sultan. You also have friends in Jewel Hill. You can convince Verona. She may . . .'

'Stop . . . stop . . . stop!' I jerked my arm free and screamed with each word louder than the previous one, as my nails automatically reached and started scratching my face.

'Ohhh . . . Cyntha! What have you done?' my heart cried. I felt as if I had been thrown back into the dreadful past. Verona – the name pierced my foggy chest sheltering my timid past and made it bleed.

Cyntha was shocked to encounter the reality, to find that the person who she was expecting would be her infallible hero was in reality a coward villain.

She ran out of the room crying, as I remained all alone at the window trying to drape back my stripped and wounded past.

All preparations had been made.

I looked around the dark and deserted oasis from the window of my room and quietly questioned the moon. It duly assured me that everyone in the Last Step was fast asleep.

Now, the only thing required was to pick my bag and walk inaudibly for a few metres.

I was not anxious. I knew I would not wake anyone up. I was a master escapist – behave absolutely normal throughout the day; make sure to eat, make sure your face does not yield 'goodbye' emotions and make sure your heart is locked and chained and is in no position to be able to communicate with your knees. That is it and no one will ever know that they were nursing a dodger in their company.

There was no point in meeting and explaining to Cyntha that for me to go back into that world would be worse than death and that I was the worst choice to be sent to the heavens' gates to plead with the annoyed gods.

I put my hand into my pocket and took out something that had always been with me since the day I left the island – a broken piece of a mirror. No, do not think that I was keeping it to see how I aged.

I hadn't seen my face for years.

I was using this mirror as some sort of a curing remedy and to use it for that purpose was simple. Whenever I was reminded of my past I looked into it and . . . spat.

Yes, spat.

Again, do not think that I hated my face.

No.

This was the only way to release the obstinate venom that was trapped in my veins. And trust me it worked.

My fingers moved over its abrasive surface as I thanked the mirror. I remained with it for a long time before putting it back and walking in the darkness towards my only piece of luggage – a hand-stitched bag made of my old, torn clothes.

As my hand clutched the bag, I felt something fall.

I bent to pick it up but was astonished at what I saw – a few notes lay on the floor exactly in the same manner as they did on the night of my first escape.

My body slumped to the ground, my eyes kept staring at the money as my mind took me back to my valley.

Mother's entire savings?

What would she have thought the next day?

How would she be now?

Would she still be hopeful?

Would she still be alive?

Oh! mother, my heart lamented, why did you not stop me? You could have at least come and said goodbye?

Suddenly my mind turned to Cyntha. She too knew that I was about to flee but did the same.

Why did she not say anything?

Why did she leave the money?

Why?

Did she think so lowly of me?

Even though the moon kept pestering me to leave, I remained there, frozen, for a long time, until my head fell with disgrace.

Thirty-four

~

She had woken up earlier than usual.
Maybe to confirm whether I had left, but could not believe what her misty eyes saw in the weak light of dawn.

There I was, sitting in one corner of the barn's corridor across the Headmaster, flipping through his fund-seeking proposal!

'I will need to read it,' although I had realised her presence, I addressed the Headmaster without looking at Cyntha.

'However, I still believe finding a wilful benefactor will be no less than a miracle.' I added.

I knew she was there, standing at the door but after the night's incident I just could not gather the strength to look at her, not even to see that her face was now glowing with happiness.

But why was she happy?

Did she seriously believe that I was capable of doing something?

Perhaps she did; but Cyntha's blind faith was not unfamiliar to me. I had seen it long before in someone Cyntha reminded me of most.

I looked at the report attentively. Thanks to the time spent in Ira's classroom, it was easy for me to make sense of it.

I had never imagined that one day my part-time occupation would eventually take such an important role in somebody else's life.

I stayed in the corridor for hours, discussing and noting down the intricacies of cash flows. I was surprised that I still remembered what I had learnt from Ira.

I know I am leaving many questions unanswered, for instance –

Why in spite of my shattered state did I decide to stay back?

Why, when I knew that going back to the world of true pearls would be inviting more humiliation, did I agree to return?

Why, when I thought securing funding was an impossible exercise, did I still undertake the job?

Honestly, I do not have convincing answers.

Maybe, I was too scared to break that blind faith again.

However, I had only decided and to decide was one thing and doing it was another. I was still unsure how I would prepare myself for the task.

After meeting the old woman of the mela and having lived under the shadow of the open hood it was impossible to undertake anything insignificant with exuberance. I had come to know that anything that had no grand goal, anything that was not eventually related to attaining the status of a true pearl was meaningless to pursue. And these thoughts returned as soon as my mind started working. What difference does it make to the world that in one of its remote corners, in one small oasis, one man wants to save a dying school?

As for that, consider the case of the unknown Headmaster—someone sleeping in my mind for years suddenly woke up and argued—who would ever remember that he was the one who went all the way to the river to meet the king?

I stopped writing and looked at the Headmaster; he was a native of the desert and was my age but with a scorched face, tired eyes, hesitant frame – as if the harsh wind of the desert had snatched his youth from him. Instinctively my hand touched my own face. Did it look the same, tiresome... undefined... lonely, I wondered. 'Why not...?' I heard somebody hiding in one corner of my mind saying '... aren't all dummy pearls supposed to look the same?' I kept looking at the Headmaster until the expressions on his face changed and broke my reverie. Everything else is a tether, the old words kept slithering around my ears, as I lowered my head and tried hard to listen to the beaten voice of the Headmaster.

Thirty-five

~

I entered the large gates of the school and was amazed at the sight.

The king of the desert truly knew the art of earning immortality.

Standing with its back to miles and miles of nothingness, right at the end of a gigantic rectangular ground, the magnificent stony structure looked capable of lasting for hundreds of years.

It was rectangular shaped and was surmounted by a huge dome and surrounded by four towers at its four corners. An immensely long finial stood erect at the top of the dome pointing towards the skies as if wanting to reach the heavens!

But that was not all that made the school look astonishing. It was those two identical human faces, presumably of the king of the desert, chiselled out of two huge white rocks and resting on large pedestals on both sides of the building.

I remained near the entrance staring at the protruding faces which appeared as if they were desperate to come alive and shout, 'Look and remember us, as we are the faces of the great king who once owned this desert!'

Just as I was busy admiring the king's feat, the school bell rang and out came hundreds of children running, filling the rectangular ground.

Suddenly, the place started looking different.

It was a great contrast– poverty dancing with those silent wealthy kings in the backdrop.

Those hunger-ridden yet smiling faces appeared in that satisfied structure exactly as a beggar's food would look on a shining silver plate.

But now the tasteless food was to be thrown away, it seemed it was some kind of a conspiracy of the privileged structure which perhaps never liked the constant presence of suffering children in its capable veins.

ॐ

My next two days were spent at the school understanding its working and simultaneously encouraging the children of the desert not to lose hope.

I did not know how successful I was, as their quiet faces said nothing. Maybe they were too naïve or maybe they knew it all!

However, all my doubts cleared when the day of my departure came.

I needed to start early as the journey was too long and the time the children had, too short.

The desperate sun was waiting around the corner, as I packed my bags and finally looked into the mirror.

Instinctively, a hollow smile ran on my face as I had caught the mirror red-handed which now looked helpless, wanting to hide in shame.

The poor mirror that was once the most important reference in my life knew that it had no value now, as it was beaten by my speculation of my appearance and in spite of its great efforts was not able to show me worse.

I heaved a sigh and picked my baggage before moving towards the barn's exit. I stepped out and could not believe what my eyes saw.

The barren ground was full of children and villagers and nobody needed to tell me what they all were waiting for!

I turned and looked at Cyntha, who stood near the corridor brimming like the rising sun.

One by one they all came forward, some to wish me luck, some to bless me, some to tie good luck charms on my arm, as my eyes went back in time to clear dust from the damaged porch of the old church to show me what remained engraved there in spite of the renovation:

Fortunate are those who are trusted more by others than by themselves;
Blessed are those who trust others more than they trust themselves.

Thirty-Six

~

I did not realise when the oases passed, when the slender river began and when it turned into an enormous ocean.

And it all happened because those hundreds of faithful eyes had taken me back to the days when I was a little boy, a time when everything I did, I did to please my mother. A time when it did not bother me whether I spent days doing something as silly as taking cows for grazing. *'One day you yourself will turn into an ox'*, my shopkeeper uncle used to mock me, but I never cared... until I entered the mela.

And as if those childhood days of cow grazing had returned, now it did not affect me that the work that I was doing would one day be buried in the white dunes of the desert.

I just wanted to do it because it meant something to someone.

And as I once spent my days reading out my textbooks to Saviour, I spent my entire journey working on the fund proposal as if Ira was around, sitting beside me, checking it and giving instructions – *put a zero there... put a comma here ...no, wait... it looks too complex... let's convert this proposal into a simple story.*

As the cargo ship headed towards the Island carrying its only passenger, I repeatedly watched the rising and the setting of the sun and the period of the moon in-between. Strangely, it really felt that they both did share some kind of arrangement and Ira's words about the moon being dearer to God appeared to be somewhat true. After all, the punctual son, the sun, was always eager to rise and set and was never given any liberty whereas the moon came and went at its own will and also got away with straying from the rules – changing its size whenever it pleased and time and again, coming out during the day to taunt its brother.

And one day as the water changed its colour and there was the same unique fragrance in the wind, I realised that the time had come to encounter the dangerous cobra again.

My hand instinctively rose and touched the grey streaks in my hair and my ordinary attire, as I remembered those with whom I had once pledged to enter the heavens only through its front gates.

Who would have believed that one out of the three of us would get imprisoned by his veiled destiny for years only to be released with no other option but to enter the heavens through its back door?

I smiled faintly and slowly moved towards the harbour.

※

Having walked up the Jewel Hill from the entry at the back, I stood inside the heavens awestruck, wearing the outfit of a servant and a happy expression painted on my face, as my eyes refused to believe what they encountered!

'Heaven', now I realised was the perfect term used for Jewel Hill. After all, isn't the term 'heaven' used for a place that man cannot create?

I had only heard that man wanted to build towers which would reach the skies, but now my eyes were actually seeing them.

Each building in Jewel Hill was in the shape of a tower, each of which was made of bricks of gold and was taller than the tallest thing I had ever seen. And each unbelievably had managed to pierce the sky!

Nothing was impossible for these true pearls, who, when they could not reach the sky, had brought it down!

Yes! The Jewel Hill had its own sky – a semi-oval wrap that acted at nobody else's but their command. They said drizzle! And it started drizzling ! They said stars! And the stars started twinkling!

So 'heaven' is what the open hood was rightly called. Tell me, could all these be created by man ... if yes, why doesn't he create such prosperity in every land?

There were no roads in Jewel Hill, just clouds floating, carrying people from one place to another. It suited the heavens, after all who would want to walk on the firm surface of reason and come out of that dreamy paradise?

However, nothing could beat what my eyes were just witnessing.

Right in the centre of Jewel Hill, the true pearls had created a huge replica of the *Rings* and filled it with statues.

The *left side* had a cluster of life-size statues of wax all standing haphazardly near each other ... all with similar faces, similar clothes, similar height, looking like nothing but exact copies of each other.

But the enormously tall wax statues on the *right side* were worth seeing. It had everyone—from the king who visited our valley to the king who ruled the desert—the actors, the footballers, the merchants, the leaders; every true pearl that the world had seen till now. Each of these statues was decorated with the most expensive jewellery and clothing and each sculpted with such precision that made them appear almost real.

And right in front of everyone in the *Rings* stood the wax statue of Geoga and Verona with these words carved on the chest of my childhood friend – *In the magical Island of True Pearls, the year it rained the most, even before I turned eighteen, I became a king.*

Their eyes stared at me and their faces bore a proud smile. I tried to stand tall on my toes and match their immeasurable height but still could not compete with it!

The bygone years have made my *friends* the tallest! Geoga has emerged as the most expensive actor in history and Verona, the most glitzy.

Their miniature models now sold in thousands as most sought-after toys at the windows of every shop on the street of mirrors.

I stood for a long time near the *Rings* admiring the heavens and remembering what my mother said once – *God feels safe in the mountains*. Oh Mother! You were always right. Where else on earth, can God think of residing?

❧

Heavens is heavens only for its owners, not for those who serve there, is what I realised within a few days.

To be even in the vicinity of the true pearls was impossible, let alone seeking funding from them. We were servants and our purpose was to keep our masters happy, not bother them with fanciful demands.

However, unbelievably, one of the true pearls had agreed to listen to my request.

I kept walking pointlessly through the clouds thinking about the gamble I had taken while faintly glancing at the chariots passing by.

It was difficult to keep staring at those flashing lights that emerged from the cloudy streets every now and then.

No, these did not come from the headlights of chariots or something else; these got emitted whenever a true pearl rode by, with the window of the chariot open.

I had only seen these true pearls from a distance yet could not keep my eyes focused on their faces for more than a moment – each of the true pearls in the heavens had a halo surrounding their face, emitting radiant rays. The richer the true pearl, the stronger their glow.

Lost in my thoughts, I did not realise when I left the cloudy streets and reached a dense forest-like area. Like all other things in heaven, it too appeared larger than life – too orderly, too complete, too picturesque.

Instinctively, my feet turned towards the interiors in search of more seclusion. I had not walked far when I saw that strange structure – a huge, shabby looking building with no windows and no entrance, looking like a huge cardboard box standing in the middle of the woods.

Even its surroundings looked very unlike heaven – scattered rocks, untrimmed shrubs and muddy roads with small burrows all over... as if somebody had dug the place up in search of a hidden treasure.

I had heard from the other servants that the structure was known as mad-house. A place that housed the troublemakers of Jewel Hill – the true pearls who strangely, all of a sudden, started disliking the grandeur of Jewel Hill, its piercing towers, its golden streets. Now and then, one such true pearl would leave his tower and charge towards the streets with a pickaxe, throwing gold bricks at the moving cars and hurling abuses at the artificial sky. He would refuse to go back into his tower and would only calm down when brought to the mad-house.

I kept looking at the mad-house, the odd one out, while my mind kept warning me of the consequences I could now face in the next few days.

My days on Jewel Hill had slipped faster than I had imagined and nothing had come through except the anticipated insults, rejections and threats.

And so I took that gamble.

Especially after that frightful dream.

The dream in which I saw myself dressed as a native of the desert walking slowly through the hot nothingness, strangely, leading a caravan.

A caravan that comprised only of the children of the Last Step.

A caravan that had no camels, no luggage, no camping material yet it moved definitively on an invisible path.

We kept walking for a long time when I saw myself requesting the children to stop as I was tired and wanted to rest. And then as I slept on the blistering sand and the children waited quietly facing the prickling gust of sand, a huge sandstorm rose from nowhere and moved rapidly towards us. The children panicked and tried to wake me up but my eyes refused to open. I knew that one by one the cruel sandstorm was snatching the children away from me but I remained like a lifeless piece of wood slowly being buried under the sand!

The dream ended but left its scar.

Did the sandstorm come only because I went to sleep?

I knew the days of the school were numbered and something had to be done.

And so I did what could be done.

I sent my report to the great actor Geoga reminding him of the days we spent as childhood friends.

And as if he did remember everything, I got an answer.

I was given the opportunity by my very own Geoga to present my case in his palatial court.

I knew our encounter could spell disaster for me.

But then, what could threaten a man, who could not be killed even by the most poisonous venom?

Thirty-seven

~

Trying to memorise all the facts about the school, the nervous nobody stood below the True Geoga.

The glittering Geoga!

The majestic Geoga!

The Geoga, who started his life at the very same box on the snake and ladder board as me, but what heights had he attained and at what lows had I remained....

The only consoling factor was that both our lives were free from the clutches of that silly snake and ladder game – he had climbed every ladder and was way up on the board and ironically, after being bitten by every snake, I had altogether refused to play the game.

I raised my head and tried looking at the dazzling face of Geoga who sat far up on a two storied, high chair along with two of his friends, one very fat and the other very thin sitting on similar chairs.

And I stood in front of them—far below on the ground—waiting for my turn to speak.

It was one of the hundreds of rooms of his regal palace where the king Geoga was holding his court.

I glanced through one of the windows at the gardens outside where countless cameras waited for him to come out and show them his face... or his hand, or his finger or whatever they had in their destiny today.

'So,' Geoga spoke loudly looking casually into the proposal, 'what do my able assistants have to say about this?'

As Geoga spoke, a gong sounded and out came four wise-looking men from nowhere, two carrying a huge machine on their shoulders and two a big bundle of what looked like filed papers.

While I tried hard to come to terms with the strange proceedings, one of the four wise men instantly started as if he himself was the machine, 'The equation is falling short, God!'

He looked gravely at the pile of papers and continued, 'Total money spent on the mere education of three thousand five hundred and fifty two units at a distance of seven thousand three hundred and seventy seven miles from the cameras, over a period of several years; when compared to the amount of fame generated falls terribly short in terms of the rate of return. To simplify, who sees when a peacock dances inside a deep forest?'

He stopped as if somebody had turned the switch off.

Silence prevailed as the wise man ended his analysis.

'Hmmm' after heaving a long pensive sigh, Geoga slowly turned his head towards the very fat man and posed a question, 'Who can know about money more than the wealthiest person of Heavens?'

The fat man gave a sarcastic nod before opening his mouth, 'I think the project is worth funding. Why only funding? We will give hundred percent employment guarantee on top of it,' he spoke while playing with some marbles in his hands pretending to be serious. He may not have realised but I had recognised him – the young face of the fat boy who ran with us from the yellow valley could still be seen behind those enhanced layers of fat.

'Every child who studies from our school...,' he raised his voice as if making an announcement, '...will get a seven generation job contract to work in the wonderful Giant Wheel of the *MoneyGate*.'

He then turned his head towards the very thin man and questioned sardonically while joining his hands, 'Oh most powerful person in the Heavens! Can there be a better act of charity than that?'

The thin man who was dressed like a sage replied in a sage-like tone, 'I do not know about us but this man definitely has an opportunity to become immensely famous in and around that oasis.'

Yes, Geoga hadn't forgotten anything, neither our friendship nor what happened on his wedding day.

I was not summoned for money but to hand the punishment that had long been due. 'Hmmm, so the money is actually for him,' Geoga continued with his forged sincerity.

'How selfish!' he mocked and threw the proposal on the ground.

I was stunned. All my preparations, my figures, my answers, my arguments, now lay there, licking the dust. And so did my false hopes.

I prepared to leave, thinking that the court was adjourned but no, the final ruling was yet to come.

'Stop!' the judge Geoga hissed.

'Listen to this before you go, you defeated man! You were beaten because you were nowhere near the great Geoga in terms of acting.' He thumped his chest and raised his voice, 'Yes, the magical Geoga! Do you want to know why? Because you missed the most important lesson of acting. Yes, the most important. Cleverness. Yes, cleverness. Think and you will realise. Who is the greatest actor? The one who shows his skill in the theatres? No, the greatest actor is the one who can act in real life. Who can convince you that he is your greatest friend, your most beloved lover. Oh, foolish dummy pearl! Go back to your unknown world and never ever think of returning to our heaven!'

And with this final verdict the court was adjourned. The three gods came down to earth and stormed out of the door leaving the convict of the day mourning his imprudence.

'In a way he is right,' this was all the offender could think of, 'maybe it was cleverness. . . .'

As everyone left and I remained alone in that high-roofed room, two important things happened – one, it suddenly struck me that the agony of this insult was far less than my expectation. No, actually it was the other way round.

Interestingly, I felt a strange sense of firmness blended with subtle happiness deep in my heart, maybe my subconscious mind was pleased that I was now strong enough to confront any calamity; or maybe, I had got the clue of what had been missing and what I needed to do in the next few minutes, as, all of a sudden I rose and ran towards the gardens, leaving my proposal behind . . . it was not needed anymore in the drama that was about to unfold.

'I express my gratitude towards the great master Geoga!' I shouted and pierced through the crowd of flashing cameras to reach the three gods like a faithful servant.

It happened all at once and took even the genius Geoga by surprise. I faced the cameras with my clasped palms, knowing fully well that I was right in front of the eyes of people.

'The renowned star does not like anyone to know about his benevolent nature but how can we minions, who benefit from his deeds hold back our gratefulness?' I spoke in a loud voice and bent myself.

The words coming out of my mouth were flawless, and why not, I had a great experience of working without a written script in one such important scene.

The cameras were absorbed and the expressions on the judges' face perfect for the shot. They all knew that this time all constituents of the important equation were well in place.

'Pardon me, true pearl,' I bowed my head and continued, 'but the people must know that the compassionate Geoga has graciously funded one of the most *interesting* charity projects of the world.'

Interesting? Yes, that was another component of the equation that had fallen short, mere education of children in even the remotest part of the world was not interesting enough and this word was very important in order to keep the cameras attentive.

'Yes, the most interesting,' I repeated and raised my volume even further and my eyes expressed immense happiness as if they had encountered a hidden treasure. 'An extraordinary school, hidden from the rest of the world, deep inside the desert! A school where every child has the potential to become a true pearl. Yes, you heard it right, a star! They are exceptional yet concealed like uncut diamonds buried inside the mines and the kind Geoga, who himself had been a destitute, untapped talent once wants to bring such gifted children to the world's attention!'

As if my words had magical powers, the cameras along with enhanced flashes started babbling, trying to outdo each other, duly suggesting that the equation was now complete.

I looked towards Geoga with a smile as if saying, cleverness? Is this what you meant, my lord?

I had heard it from the people of the desert that a mouse when caught in a perilous situation reacts aptly because it has such encounters on a daily basis whereas a lion which is rarely caught in such situations is often late in its reaction.

All cameras were now on Geoga and the other two judges and they all knew very well that a wrong statement at this moment could become costlier than even funding the entire school.

No doubt they were specialists in their game, but this time the lions were trapped in somebody else's scene.

Something had to be said and Geoga tried his best, 'It is true. This is an amazing story and we will make sure that it does not suffer by any means.'

He spoke forgetting what had happened inside the closed doors.

'But,' the once fat boy of the unknown valley and now the wealthiest man of the Heavens had got those precious moments to think and was ready to turn the tables, 'As with all such stories; to trust its authenticity, we had to draw a strategy,' he glanced towards the other two and continued, 'we have given six months to this man and his school. Take whatever you want from us,' he spoke while looking at me trying his best to hide his anger, 'but prove to us what you promised. We will all be there along with our cameras, at the end of the six months to verify the truth. Accomplishment will open the gates of heaven for you and them forever, but a failure will shut even those of hell.'

I could see the cynical smiles on their faces, as if they knew what would happen but I smiled back.

It was they who were interested in the future, being true pearls. But being a wanderer, I was now only interested in the present.

I knelt down in front of the three gods and nodded my head in acceptance, as our captured images were transmitted to the earth with lightning speed.

I visited Ira's classroom before returning to the Last Step, but could not meet her. She had gone to visit the benefactor, who was funding her school. I had lived with Ira for long, but somehow we never managed to talk about her patron. Perhaps, during those times nothing else mattered to me.

It was going to be a while before she came back but I had to be with the children as soon as possible. I knew what Ira would have done if she was in my place. So rather than waiting for her I decided to leave.

*

And so I returned; too engrossed thinking about ways to live up to my tall claims.

I do not know how many times I asked the ocean to suggest a solution but knowing the nature of the dangerous challenge I had thrown at the true pearls even the sea remained silent.

However, something had to be thought of and something had to be done, so I thought of and did something that even the kings of the desert could never have imagined.

Thirty-eight

~

Farmer's eyes
Staring at the skies
Holding the barren soil
He knew his efforts would get foiled
Yet was ready for months of toil
Farmer's eyes
Staring at the skies!

Facing an enormous crowd of children, I stood right in the middle of the two huge sculptures, on a temporarily erected stage with my hands on my waist and the head held high ... exactly like I once did near the *Rings* waiting for my turn.

I hope you did not look too closely because if you did, you would have found that like the two-faced king of the desert I, too, now had two faces!

My first face that was visible to the children had the same confident eyes and the same warrior-like smile that it did when I was fighting my last battle in the *Rings*.

But my second face, the authentic one, the nervous one, had the expression of a farmer who stands on his prepared field with seeds in his hand, knowing that it may not rain, yet has to go ahead and sow. That second face was now completely hidden behind the confident one.

I lowered myself and filled my fist with sand and gestured the children to do the same.

This was my first important interaction with them and I knew any fickleness on my part would alienate them forever. It had to be my best performance, even better than the one I had managed inside the cruel *Rings*.

I opened my palm and spoke as if I was talking to that one grain –

'Oh grain of sand,' I addressed my palm in a loud, fervent voice, 'What is it that you want to complain about?'

And then, as if I myself was that grain, I replied in a childlike voice with a touch of sadness, 'Oh, unknown visitor, just that I am nothing, nothing but a mere grain of sand. Right now, if I am blown out of your palm by this mischievous wind and get mingled in the desert, would you know which one is me out of the millions? I complain because this vast desert does not increase if I am added nor reduce, if I am taken away. Then, should not this grain question why does it have to exist at all?

Oh guest of the desert, you may not know but I spend my entire day blistering under the heat only in this hope that the night will come and relieve me from the cruel sun. Alas! The night does come but grips me with its shivering hands. I tremble, I am whirled and rolled and thrown about until that final moment when my heart eventually cries and helplessly requests the sun to open those frozen skies again. And like this my life goes on.'

I paused and looked around, my face at the front brimming with certainty but the hidden one fearfully wondering, 'Will the children understand?'

'But traveller,' the grain continued, 'Why should I be the only one to complain when sadly there are others who suffer the same pain? These children of the desert, who stand in queues listening to you, do not know, but in reality they too are like us grains of sand. They too, from generations, are born and are buried ineffectively in this thirsty desert, leaving it unchanged.'

I laughed loudly and pretended to tease the grain, 'Oh grain, I may be a traveller or a guest but I know the way through which you can separate yourself from this arid desert. Look! Here I pour water on you and watch how it changes your colour! And now even if you try you cannot mingle with the dry nothingness!'

The grain smiled and replied, 'Oh, once a traveller, but now my friend! You are clever but tell me how this one wet speck will be able to quench the thirst of such a huge desert?'

This time I did not reply to the grain but instead, looked towards the children and proclaimed like a king, 'In that case we pledge to pour water on all of us and then see who stops our desert from changing into a glittering land!'

I did not stop there, I continued forgetting that I was just acting, 'Tomorrow morning, I will wait here for every child who wants to transform this desert ... not alone ... but with his dream of what he wants to be and what he thinks he can never be.'

I stopped.

The class was over.

I did not wait for their response. It was useless. What now mattered was how many were going to turn up the next day?

❧

I sat at the window with my eyes fixed on the White Mountain that had turned crimson and was emitting golden rays.

I had shifted myself to one of the rooms of the school, the one which was situated closest to the nothingness.

The sun had crossed the White Mountain and was rolling down its back, in the process creating a halo around the mountain.

I remained seated with my eyes trying to measure the infinite height while my real face remembered the morning speech.

Would they come back? As my heart wondered, my ears heard a knock.

'You were amazing!' Cyntha chirped with excitement while entering the room. 'Never before this day could I think like this. Now I too have thought of a *dream* to which you must listen to!'

I looked at her passionate face with surprise. Suddenly a thought struck, the game was turning dangerous. What if the children did come back with their dreams, worked on it for the next six months with blind faith and eventually failed? Would they all not reach a much worse condition? Would they be able to live with that burning chest? I could not think further.

'Come, let us go for a walk,' I gestured Cyntha and moved towards the door.

I kept walking quietly towards the mountain which was changing its colour, as Cyntha followed. We had come a long way, the window was left far behind when I stopped and looked at her.

'Do you see that peak, Cyntha?' I asked pointing to the White Mountain in that dim light and continued without waiting for her response, 'I always used to look at it from the Last Step and assume that it was possible to conquer that crest but today, having walked this far I feel what I had thought is unattainable. Even if somehow one manages to climb to the top, it will be impossible to return. Our dreams are like climbing this mountain and their realisation like the return. What is the fun in climbing when you know you cannot come back?'

Cyntha remained silent. I regretted speaking as soon as I had finished. My years of isolated living had made me callous. Perhaps I was now incapable of bringing peace to anyone.

Perhaps I should have been clever with Cyntha?

Perhaps I have shattered her dream? I feared.

But no, I was wrong.

'You know what happiness really is?' Cyntha posed a question after a long silence.

I did not reply.

She continued, 'I learnt this as I grew up on water. A moment comes in every person's life when he does not want that moment to change. Not because he is not ambitious, but because his heart says that there can be nothing better. In that moment, the person may not be in the state which he had always dreamt for himself or be with the person who fits his definition of an 'ideal soul mate' but still he willingly wants to be in *that* state, with *that* person forever. Today, standing with you in the shadow of White Mountain with that one *dream* of mine in the eyes, I feel the *happiest*. It would not matter, if I am not able to realise my dream because I have already attained what I think is the happiest moment for me.'

And then Cyntha went on to tell her dream, her dream to convert that animal barn into a permanent hospital and staying in the last oasis for the rest of her life with me.

I was speechless, wondering, why had I never had such small dreams?

Thirty-nine

~

I should have guessed. Cyntha's answer was a subtle hint to what was to happen in the next six months in that sleeping oasis.

I sat in the Headmaster's room staring at the door with astonishment, as the children came and went, one by one, handing in their dreams without any interruption.

I was amazed. Who could think that such simple eyes could harbour such big dreams and that too without any mystification? Unlike me they knew what they wanted to be, maybe they had already heard the tale of the female magician and the rational master or maybe this younger generation was much ahead of my estimation of them.

I kept reading their dreams, curtailing some and elevating a few, while peeking at the children through the window, as they played freely in those dusty grounds.

I knew that each child in that courtyard believed that he could achieve what he thought and apart from their destitute eyes this self-reliance was to be my biggest weapon in the forthcoming battle.

I stayed in that room for a while before finally moving decisively towards the grounds taking one of the dreams in my hand.

'What is my beautiful Maari doing?' I asked and sat beside that little girl who was busy making a sketch on the sand.

Maari's dream was in my hands. She wanted to become a sand artist, someone who could create very large sketches, as large as the forests, the mountains, the rivers... like Mother Nature herself.

Impossible! My hidden face shouted; it knew Maari was blind.

'I am changing the colour of this sand permanently. Why take the trouble of constantly pouring water?' she smiled, mischievously.

I kept gazing at Maari as my mind went back to the time when as a child I had painted those bushes that threatened Saviour.

'People think I cannot see colours,' she continued while her small hands kept moving over the sand. 'I can, and I can tell that the colour of our sand is changing.' She said while pointing towards the nothingness, as if she could see.

'You know, Maari,' my second face did not care to hide itself, there was no need, hence my voice sounded real, 'This ground is too small for the kind of painting you do. In a few days I will take you outside the Last Step and together we will create one of the biggest paintings this world will ever see.' I got up but could very well notice that her hands were now moving much faster.

And like this, Maari became my second student, yes – second, because Sultan had already started working on his dream. He had been a trader since he was seven and had always dreamt of becoming one of the richest businessmen ever born in the desert.

'How is it possible?' while I walked with him under the scorching sun, Sultan spoke with uncertain eyes.

Sultan was an extremely sharp child who only needed some assurance. My brain worked quickly.

Who should I enact in this situation?

The answer came.

'Sultan!' I said while making a hollow fist and putting it near my ear pretending to hear something, 'Your answer is travelling in our direction and to hear it you only need to stand affixed where you are standing for the next five minutes.'

Sultan looked around and unconvincingly followed what I said.

Barely two minutes had passed, when he tried to move from his place – the straight rays falling from the burning sun were making it unbearable for him to stand at one place.

I warned with a smile, 'If you move, the answer will change its direction.'

He remained where he was but soon started raising his ankle; the sand under his feet was now pinching him like needles.

'Did you see Sultan?' I said with the same smile while gesturing him to relax, 'The wandering sun is feeble, but turns into a force the moment we fix its attention. It is all about concentrating your energy. Gather it and put it in one direction and everything is possible.'

※

It seemed that their peaceful faces accepted both happiness and sadness as the same, as nothing made them forget to assemble every night in that barren ground and sing to the desert.

I sat opposite Cyntha looking at her through the flames as we all gathered around the bonfire. Slowly their voices began to rise, their hands started to clap and my lips moved in sync as if I knew the words. That night Cyntha appeared different to me. Her face, her eyes, her lips appeared as though I was seeing them for the first time.

Sitting among the children, she looked like their mother. I continued looking at her when all of a sudden I felt that unfamiliar sense of peace inside. It lasted only for a moment but seemed like a lifetime. Since then, that moment is embedded in my mind; it was short but special.

I still remember, I had looked around then and was surprised to see everyone appearing so intimate, so friendly. I felt I had been living with them not for hundreds of years, not even for thousands, but from the time my soul came into existence.

I felt as if I was them and they were me, even the beggar, who lay inertly near the traveller's platform felt so close. For a brief moment, when I looked at his tattered blanket, I saw not him but me sleeping inside it. I felt as if it was not him, but me who lived his entire life resting unresponsively on those grains of sand.

But that moment ended as abruptly as it came, as somebody entered my mind to snatch that peace away, to fill it with fire. It was that old woman of the mela, who appeared out of the bonfire to show me melting dummy pearls and then the screaming children, all looking at me and pleading for help. I quickly rose and with swift steps walked out of the oasis. I did not slow down but kept walking deep into the nothingness until the fainting lights stopped their chase.

I think songs heard in special moments are magical, as, without letting you know they possess your tongue making it repeat them.

I kept walking barefoot on the cold sand and kept humming the song that I used to sing a lot during my preparation days on the Island; to encourage myself, to tell myself that even if I have to die, I would not stop.

I was so caught up in infusing enthusiasm in myself that I committed the gravest mistake which even a child of the desert would never commit – to enter unprotected into its dark, freezing expanse.

I looked around with panic. I knew it was not about surviving one night, it was likely that with no instrument of navigation, food and water, I would never be able to return to the settlement.

Suddenly, a smile spread across my face. I hadn't turned mad, it was just that I remembered the times when I had entered the desert with the sole purpose of dying and how in a few months, so much had changed that now I was just not ready to give up my life.

I sat down.

Even in those taxing moments my heart could not stop itself from thinking about Ira. Slowly, the panic subsided.

It was not long before my ears heard somebody's footsteps. I turned and was surprised to find a young boy standing unperturbed in such loneliness.

The boy's face looked familiar; I had seen it often in those dusty grounds of my school.

'My name is Noora,' the boy introduced himself, 'I was sent after you by the Headmaster. It is fatal to walk into the desert like this. The wind here is changing.' He paused for a moment and looked towards the sky before continuing, 'Let's get out of here quickly.' He finished and started walking. I followed swiftly.

I was amazed at Noora's confidence, he knew exactly in which direction to walk. I looked at his empty hands and confident feet and asked, 'Can you see what I can't see, Noora?'

He smiled and spoke, 'People call me the "eyes of the desert".' He said with a sense of pride, 'Leave me anywhere in the desert, blindfold me if you want, still I will find my way back home.'

'How do you do that?' I asked while my hand slowly slipped into my pocket to take out my students' list of dreams.

'Do not tell anyone, I can talk to these stars,' he pointed towards the clear sky and said, 'They have their own language which I understand very well.'

Surprised at Noora's accurate knowledge of constellations, I probed further, 'And how long can you talk to these stars?'

'For my entire life,' Noora smiled and replied, 'If the sun does not rise in between.'

I smiled back. Maybe it was not that bad a thing to enter the desert at night, after all it was because of this I had met my third student. I took out a pen and wrote 'Youngest astronomer in the world' next to his name, as my eyes saw those murky lights again.

Forty

~

It all started with one camel and a few travellers.

They pitched their tents near the edge of the school and stayed all day watching me and my children.

As usual, I began with a sermon of dreams assuring the children of the desert that in no way were they lesser than the world they had never seen.

With each passing day, the list of dreams was getting elongated. Just yesterday it had seen the 'best archers' along with the names of many footballers, actors, singers, athletes, dancers, boxers....

'Do you know what all has been given to our world by the people of the desert?' I said the moment someone looked uncertain. *The first magnificent structure. The first surgery. The decimal system. The oldest civilisation.*

And that incident with the kite flyer whose kite touched the skies?

Do you like talking to the skies? I asked.

I think the sky only extends as far as my kite goes! He answered in a disappointed tone.

Go to the world beyond the kite
Touch the stars, big and bright.

The 'string' is only when you feel
It is the fear that makes you kneel
You can, yes, you can!

I sang to assure the 'best paraglider of the world' along with the other dreamers.

I had assumed that the travellers would leave the next day, but was little surprised to see an increase in their number. Their unfastened, straw-munching camels and the unhurried earthen pots resting on the smoke-exhaling twigs suggested that they were here to stay.

And stay they did.

With each day, their numbers rose and added to the large swarm of people who now permanently dwelt near the school only to watch the ongoing activity with bewilderment.

But now it could be called anything but a school. Its rectangular ground never looked as perplexing as it looked then – scores of unchiselled, large white rocks scattered all over and thousands of practising children amidst hundreds of long poles. Besides, there were countless unrecognisable forms on which numerous workers worked day in and day out.

It looked disorganised, it looked outlandish and nobody knew what I had in mind but I knew exactly what I was doing and how the place was to look in the end. 'A canvas looks the worst in its unfinished state' is what I replied to anyone who questioned me about it.

※

And as if what was happening in the Last Step was not sufficient, one day some laden strangers came riding on the dry gust of the desert. Their baggage contained not clothes, not shoes but long barricades, a cemented airfield, a moving palace and what not.

Like magicians, they kept putting their hands inside their hat and pulling out every little thing without which it was impossible for true pearls to exist.

As they went on with their act, my eyes kept staring, questioning the invaders, 'Where is that Kingsway that was once a jagged road or that new bridge over Saviour or that renovated church, which you once brought so forcefully into the unknown valley?'

I ran here and there – sometimes on the white trails of my village, sometimes on the nonexistent streets of the Last Step, sometimes on the rolling hills, sometimes on the grainy lands, but it felt the same, as if the king was coming to my small village again.

But this time I had not meant to escape but to stand and face it.

༄

I walked with anxious eyes next to the bending barricades.

The day of the arrival was not far away and the fact that I had a blank dream in my pocket was not comforting. I paused a short distance away and looked at his unobtrusive face. With more or less effort, every child in the school had been persuaded to share and to start living his dream, but this particular boy's paper had always returned blank.

I had never heard him speak to anyone; for hours he sat in one corner of the ground staring at the crest of the White Mountain. I did not know what he wanted, maybe, he was too shy or maybe he could not dream, but that day I had decided that I would not return empty-handed.

I was determined to sell him a few dreams and somehow convince him to become my final student.

As my feet moved, somebody touched my shoulder lightly. I turned around.

It was the Headmaster.

'His name is Dua,' the Headmaster knew what I was about to do, 'Nobody knows who Dua is, even this name has been given to him by the people of Last Step.'

He paused and pointed his finger towards the White Mountain, 'Do you know what is behind that imposing whiteness?' he questioned.

Finding me speechless, he continued, 'The Passage of Death,' he repeated, 'Yes, The Passage of Death. A passage where life walks solely at the mercy of cruel death.'

Instead of widening, my eyes tried to shut themselves, perhaps they had anticipated that what they were about to see was something beyond their ability to bear.

As I remembered the words of the oarsman about life around White Mountain, my ears heard those horrifying sentences, 'The desert which you have seen until now is nothing compared to the desert that exists beyond that enormous White Mountain. With far fewer oases, life in that vast desert hovers around poverty and starvation. And in such circumstances, when on the other side of the White Mountain, outsiders come with the dream that the children of the desert will be taken to rich countries, where they will be able to live comfortably by serving wealthy people, many parents give in.

'These parents do not know or maybe do not want to know that their children have to pass through many life-threatening passages before they are able to cross the boundaries of that massive desert.

'These outsiders are clever; they know that when facing such treacherous conditions many children might be tempted to return to their parents hence they remain glued to them.

'But even these merciless outsiders are powerless in front of this severe desert as there are passages which are very difficult to cross and in those situations these heartless people leave the children on their own.

'They operate in groups, one group leaves the children at the entry point of such a passage and another waits at the exit to receive them. The Passage of Death is the most difficult passage of their route, with a mountain impossible to cross on one side and a desert extending infinitely on the other.

'Each day, hundreds of children walk behind the White Mountain unaccompanied and as they walk through that dreadful path all of them sense that not many will make it to the other side and hence, when the situation worsens some of them turn towards the mountain with the hope to reach our oasis, but soon their hope turns out to be a false one, as the more they climb, the more they realise what a great mistake they have committed.

'This mountain has never spared anyone, except . . . ' Headmaster paused and sighed, 'Dua was found in an unconscious state in our desert. People say he was left there by God, as for a human to cross that White Mountain is beyond imagination.'

The frightful glimpse was over, but I remained numb. The Headmaster had spoken mere words, but my eyes had converted them into a vision and had exactly shown me what was happening behind the mountains – thirsty, starving children slithering through a rocky passage with one eye on their lost destination and the other on the invisible peak. A passage marked with small skeletons, a passage where a traveller could only sit under a leafless tree for shadow, drink white sand imagining it to be water.

And then the scene changed, I saw a few young children falling one by one and converting into corpses as they desperately tried to climb. I begged my eyes to stop but they kept showing it to me until I fell down on my knees and as if the wind too was on Dua's side, it came from nowhere and blew the blank dream away from my hands.

Forty-one

~

The appearance of that first camera had made me realise, how close I was to facing the venom again.

Under the densely clouded, dark sky I sat mesmerised, up on the school roof, near the giant dome, looking towards the glittering Last Step.

With the rise of the sun the next day, our lease of six months was to be over.

A few strokes of the night were what now separated me from my beautiful snake.

One would wonder why I took the pain to climb such heights when what had been achieved already appeared breathtaking even to the thousands present on the ground!

Do not worry, I was not running away from my promise. It was just that I wanted to be sure how exactly my theatre appeared to those coming from the skies.

And as I kept looking underneath, a smile crossed my lips instinctively. Yes, the show had not begun yet my lips had realised that what the visitors from the heavens were about to see was inconceivable even for their capable eyes – if their airfield looked big, Maari's painting, strategically chosen to be right next to it, looked much bigger.

And, as if that was not enough, an unusual sparkling necklace made up of hundreds of human faces chiselled out of huge white rocks encircled the entire Last Step. Oh! they were my Sultans and my Maaris, who now were no longer a mere grain of sand, which could be blown away just like that, instead, they had been engraved permanently over the desert, to be admired, to be talked about by the coming generations!

I turned my gaze towards the transformed, well-lit rectangular ground, the one which now held countless other things which were more astonishing, more enthralling than those two eye-catching faces of the desert king – if there was a track for camels to race on, there was also a glider for a child to fly; a football ground, boxing rings, long poles and everything else that my children needed in order to perform.

And amidst these structures, shining under the light of hundreds of lit torches, my sparkling children were present.

Who could say looking at their poised faces that they were any less than the ones from the *three gates*!

They were practising, simultaneously roaring and waving towards the crowd when all of a sudden I realised that I no longer had two faces but just one.

The one that now was full of confidence.

Actually, confidence is a modest word; I felt as if there was no blood in my veins but lava, as if I was a giant lion and the last oasis my territory.

It was magical!

I felt like a sun which could shine until eternity or a storm which could engulf anything. I felt as if I could enter into the body of each child and perform whatever I wanted with utmost perfection.

I had been away from the *Rings* for years but I was certain that if I were to compete with Geoga now, I would beat him hands down. Why only acting, I felt I could now paint, dance, run, fly or even sing with perfection.

I was surprised! It was a feeling of infinite strength. Limitless. Absolutely limitless! Never in my life, had I had that kind of feeling.

My concentration broke, as my feet throbbed with mild vibration beneath. I turned my eyes and spread them over the nothingness. Miles away in the darkness, the wind was alive with a horde of fireflies that was slowly nearing the Last Step in unison.

'They are all coming to see you,' she said while sitting beside me.

It was Cyntha.

'No, Cyntha! They are arriving to see the residents of heaven!' I answered with slight resistance.

'No,' Cyntha denied with a strong shake of her head, 'They are least interested in them. They are coming to see *you* ... the man who they believe can turn this barren desert fertile. They are coming to see you perform the miracle.'

I stayed silent.

'I know you and the children will win tomorrow. And then you all will be flown back like kings to Jewel Hill, where no Geoga will be able to match you and hundreds of Veronas will queue to marry you.'

I gave a faint smile. Cyntha surely had no idea how gory the *Rings* can become on the day of the challenge.

We sat there for a long time admiring the bejewelled Last Step ... as if we were its parents and it was our child.

Suddenly, a strange feeling ran through my heart. I immediately turned my head and stared at Cyntha.

I was amazed. In one face of hers, I could now see the reflection of three people!

Mother.

Ira.

And Cyntha herself.

All looking towards me with a fulfilling smile.

I kept staring at the three faces until Cyntha got up. 'They could be here anytime. I will go down and start the preparations to welcome them,' she said and moved towards the stairs.

'And yes,' she paused and added with a touch of melancholy, 'Whenever you find time, do come and visit the Last Step. This desert will always embrace you with open arms.'

She turned her back.

I stayed behind but my eyes moved, trailing her like a honeybee.

Slowly, she walked across the ground, stopping on her way, encouraging the children, as my heart started to ponder.

Once the sun sets tomorrow, what will I do?

What do I want to do?

But . . . will we be victorious?

Why not? The first principle of acting says that you have to live the character in your mind. And hence, I am the one who will emerge as the winner tomorrow.

So, Winner! What will be your eventual destination?

Is there a doubt?

Yes. There is. Otherwise our conversation would have stopped.

A short period of silence.

I know where *I* will end up.

Where?

I will close my eyes and show you in a minute. After all, to be able to direct the heart, where it eventually should lead us, is the ultimate display of the strength of one's mind.

...Or is it the other way round? My eyes closed, but not before my heart whispered.

※

My eyes opened, as I found myself amidst dense clouds... marching like a true pearl!

Nobody needed to tell me that I had reached the top of a hill... a very tall one.

I moved, piercing the dense clouds holding my head high, trying to spot those infinitely lofty golden towers... those astonishingly real giant statues of wax.

Soon, my eyes began to narrow due to the dazzling golden rays coming through the blanket of cloud and my gaze falling on the faintly appearing heads of statues. I knew the *Rings* of heavens were near.

I looked inside myself, as if telling the heart – Did I not tell you? It had to be Jewel Hill!

And as if it was my heart's reply, slowly, the clouds started thinning down and showed me as a young boy... standing with a flute clutched in my tender hand in front of the *Rings*, yes the same *Rings* that I saw in Jewel Hill but this time... with one difference.

This time its occupants had exchanged positions!!!

On the *left side* were the Geogas, the Veronas, the fat men with all their glittering dresses, their sparkling diamonds, their painted faces... all standing one behind the other, in perfect order, stacked on the basis of the last decimal of their glitter, but as inert, as motionless as dummies, as if somebody had taken out the spirits out of their bodies!

And on the *right side* stood the Iras, the Cynthas, the caring wives, the dutiful sons, the loving daughters... standing as a group, as a bonded cluster... exactly like the extras did in the *Rings* of Jewel Hill; not inert, not motionless but very much alive. What great sage, what little saint, they all stood beside each other, equal to each other!

Amazed by this encounter I raised my head and looked around... only to find myself surrounded by numerous, shining white rocky peaks of the White Mountain!

My lips curved with a mystic smile, as words of my mother about the mighty mountains came back.

And in those very moments when I felt closest to my heart, I heard the skies burst.

One by one, those thundering airships touched the soil of the last oasis and out came the most dazzling true pearls of all categories – the Geogas, the fat men, the Veronas... one after the other... wrapped in their radiating attire... with that strong halo around.

I remained inert on the roof, absolutely unruffled, overseeing their arrival with that same mystic smile transfixed on my face.

If it had been any other time I would have warned Cyntha, who was the first in the queue that had promptly gathered to greet the glittering queen. I would have cautioned Cyntha to get out of the way of the shining true pearl that was capable of making everyone around her invisible. *Look at her countless diamonds, her large ring, her radiant skin*, I otherwise would have said, *move aside as nobody has ever escaped from the strike of a true pearl.*

Instead, I remained as still as a stone, confident and blissful, as Verona walked towards Cyntha with her glittery self.

Verona kept coming closer to Cyntha but her lustre failed to overpower its prey!

Cyntha, whose face now had strong reflections of all three faces, dazzled with a much stronger glow... so much so that in the storm of Cyntha's radiance, Verona, the queen Verona simply disappeared!!! And so did all the other faces behind her that now looked no different but exactly similar to each other!

I remained still with my eyes enthralled and my lips whispering, 'Oh, Cyntha! a *True Dummy*, you may be an anonymous, a *dummy* pearl to the flies but truly a glittering *true* pearl in the most important pair of eyes – HIS eyes.'

My eyes were now sparkling and the smiling lips were releasing those final words,

> 'Eyes truly are like blind ants, which know the way to a hidden treasure that we walk over every day ignorant of it; anyone who tames them and induces them to lead, could unearth the biggest treasure on earth. Otherwise, we all might spend our entire lives treating treasure as dust... and dust as treasure.'

Forty-two

When all the visitors of heaven went to sleep and thousands marching towards the Last Step were yet to reach it, I stood on that temporary stage, in that dark and decisive night, in front of my children, ready with my last sermon.

Until now each of my sermons had told them how to reach the status of a true pearl but my last one was to tell them what was to be done once that status was achieved.

And what could have been better than narrating to them the 'Fable of Existence'!

I concluded the fable by reminding them of my first narration and advising them that their desert needed such fulfilling 'grains' more than the already sated Jewel Hill.

I looked at them for the last time. Each one's dream was now ready to be achieved... except for Dua's. But being Ira's student how could I be satisfied with even one failure?

Yes, I had decided that I would challenge the 'Passage of Death', that I would attempt to cross the impassable White Mountain to create a passage of life, so that walking on it every child could become as fortunate, as blessed, as Dua... in a way, fulfilling the implicit dream of his.

Yes, it was an impossible task. Yes, I faced the risk of death, but then, I cared the least, after all hadn't Ira said, 'death is... when it is caused by HIM?'

Everything was to be done in a very surreptitious manner exactly as it was done on the night I escaped from my village, however, this time, everyone who loved me and whom I loved, knew precisely where I was going and why.

～

The hours of the crucial night were passing quickly, but there was still a lot to be done, after all it was to be a long and treacherous journey which could not be accomplished without the support of natives of the desert.

It was Noora, who taught me how to talk to the stars and find my way when the white desert would become dark. It was the Headmaster, who filled my backpack with supplies that were supposed to help me survive, Sultan, who taught me how to consume them prudently. It was from Maari that I learnt how to appreciate the desert with lonely eyes and to create markings on the white rocks that could last forever; from the 'camel racer', how to befriend the animals of the desert; from the 'paraglider', how to embrace heights.

One by one, they all came and shared whatever they could – how to light a fire, how to identify a storm, how to call angels of the desert for help; somebody came with the warmest of jackets, somebody with a pot of honey, somebody with the luckiest talisman.

And finally it was Dua who showed me the route that he had followed, the risks that he had encountered, the spots where he felt he would certainly die; the turns where he was fortunate;

nobody had ever seen Dua speak prior to this, that too with such excitement.

The moon was ready to vanish and so was I and for those who did not understand, my disappearance was to be as mystifying as the disappearance of the young king of the desert.

I was provided with a white horse that was trained to take people to their destination and return on its own.

The horse stood near the traveller's platform ready to take me to the foot of the White Mountain. 'Every day over the next two months, this horse will be sent to the White Mountain with the hope that it returns with you,' the Headmaster had said with a lump in his throat.

The sky was changing colour, I realised it was time to depart.

I mounted the horse and looked at Cyntha, her face was calm but her eyes were gloomy, as if asking me about her dream that had remained unattended.

I kept quiet but my eyes made my feelings evident – they were full of assurance and were continuously repeating that Cyntha's dream was now their dream and that I would surely come back and take her to the unknown valley... to introduce her to my parents... to Saviour... to my rock, which had had to wait needlessly for years.

'I will wait for you,' is all what the quivering lips of Cyntha could say to the departing cloud of sand.
Hosanna!

EPILOGUE

EPILOGUE

'Fable of Existence'

~

'Once upon a time, where now stands this White Mountain and rests this infinite desert, stood a cobra shaped island in the midst of a bottomless ocean.

And far from here, right where now flows that life-giving river, somewhere inside that vast ocean slept God.

One day, as every day, while God was peacefully asleep, his ears heard a faint sound of a cry.

He arose and opened his eyes and was surprised to see an old woman dressed in a shabby, long robe sitting in one corner of a small wooden boat and lamenting.

In spite of his consoling when the old woman refused to stop, God eventually had to ask, 'What is it that this old woman adorned with heavy ornaments want?'

'Oh, God!' the old woman joined both her hands and spoke in a sombre voice, 'Pardon me, but as you sleep here in peace the people of your island have also started living like you. Like animals, they eat, sleep and live with no motivation whatsoever to perform greater things. A creation of yours, that a man is, the one whom you blessed with extraordinary talents and abilities; isn't it a shame that he has reduced himself to this? If this animal-like behaviour is the end result, then why did you take pains in the first place to provide him with such capabilities?'

God had just opened his mouth to reply when the old woman continued with haste, 'I do not know how the others can live, but this old woman certainly cannot. And if God is capable then he should provide her with a work that challenges her and keeps her busy, otherwise here she is ready to jump into this ocean and take her life away.'

God pondered for a while and then moved his hand in the air to produce *two* rugged looking skin-bags.

'Oh, old woman!' he said while holding the two bags in his two hands, 'I have thought of a nice work for you. Take these two bags with you to the island and inspire its people to be true pearls.'

He raised his left hand and continued, 'Show them this bag, tell them to work hard, tell them to use their gifts and capabilities, tell them to raise themselves as high as they can. The more they rise, the more will be their shine and the more *fortunate* will they become.'

He raised his right hand and said, 'Show them this bag and ask them to shine in this as well. The more they think about others, the more they care about others, the more selfless they become, the more will be their shine in this one and the more *blessed* will they become.'

He handed both bags to the old woman and went back to sleep.

But then one day, as every day, while God slept peacefully, his ears heard a loud uproar.

He arose and was astonished with what his eyes could see – one of his two bags floated like an unwanted child on the water bed. He then raised his eyes and looked towards the island from where the noise was coming. He saw that the cunningness of the old woman had created mayhem.

Man had now become the most capable but in the absence of the teachings from the other bag had become the most selfish.

With angry eyes he looked at the Jewel Hill, its piercing towers; its statue of waxes; its so-called gods; the travesty of *Rings*; the suffering of the people of Crooked Tail. The more he saw, the more furious he became.

And so furious was he that he glared at the sea and the island to convert it into a desert and the Jewel Hill into a mountain of white rocks. He then captured all the true pearls-of-one-bag and converted them into shapeless white rocks and scattered them around the foot of White Mountain.

However, there were a few people who had understood the deceiving old woman and had refused to be part of her game.

And by now God's anger had also somehow subsided.

He bent to pick the bag of pearls and started walking towards the White Mountain, in the process creating oases wherever his feet rested and inhabiting all these oases with people of the Crooked Tail. He created the last oasis where once stood the *Rings*. He then created murals of the people who had refused to listen to the old woman and placed them in a circle around the last oasis.

He then summoned an old man, handed him the bag of pearls and asked him to sit with it on the peaks of the White Mountain. He drew a river in the middle of the desert and went inside.

And since then the mischievous old woman travels from village to village, carrying that one bag of pearls on her humped back, luring people to play her game. And the old man sits amidst the shining white peaks waiting for each one of us to reach him after performing in our own Last Step and climbing our own White Mountain.'